TALISMANS

ISBN 10: 1-936196-03-4
ISBN 13: 978-1-936196-03-6
LCCN: 2010928171

C&R Press
812 Westwood Ave.
Chattanooga, TN 37405

www.crpress.org

Cover and interior redesign by Lee Johnson

www.leejohnsonwriter.com

TALISMANS

SYBIL BAKER

Contents

To three who continue to inspire:
Arlene Baker
Calvin Baker (1931-2007)
Silvia Tartarini (1969-2009)

PART 1

FIREFLY

The first time: I met him the summer before kindergarten at the church choir's barbeque. The coals turned from black to gold to ash, and when I showed my mother how much they looked like the setting sun, she nodded and pulled me away from the grill so that I wouldn't burn myself.

Mark was the only other child there, cocooned between his parent's wings. His father had a shiny skull and a hairless face, too smooth to touch. His mother's gray hair fell in short waves and framed her eyes, which gazed at me from that steely place where pity and judgment live. She reached out and touched my hair, her hand heavy with honeysuckle perfume.

"You've done a great job, Beth," she said. Then she knelt down and whispered to Mark, her hand cupped so I couldn't hear. He obediently walked over to me, his hand outstretched. I can't say if he was beautiful back then.

"Go on Elise, take it." My own mother's long, thick hair was coiled in a bun and tied with a blue ribbon. Sometimes at night she let me brush and braid it. She smelled fresh, like just-washed clothes and shampoo. She peeled my fingers from her skirt and placed my hand in his. We shook hands like adults, his dirt-streaked palm damp on my skin. The adults laughed, and I burned at their condescension.

"You can let go now, Mark dear," his mother said. He dropped my hand as quickly as he had taken it. I wiped my hand on my mother's skirt, leaving a smudge I hoped she wouldn't notice.

The race: At that barbeque I challenged him. We sprinted to the tree at the other end of the churchyard, me running hard, touching the bark first. Again and again we raced as the fireflies appeared, bringing with them the smell of burning meat. Every race was close, but in the end I would pull ahead, and as soon as my fingers grazed the rough bark of the tree, I yelled that I had won. When I was twelve and knew more about those things, I challenged the boy who lived down the street to a race at our neighborhood pool. I had been winning that one, too, but in the end I pulled back.

The conversation: After dusk, Mark and I caught fireflies. From a distance the adults flitted from the red-checked table, weighted with potato salad and Jell-O molds, to the large grill, which sputtered smoke signals of distress to the world. We chased fireflies around the slope of the hill, trapped their glowing light in our cupped hands before returning them to the sky. As soon as the first star appeared, Mark sat on the grass and called me over.

"Want to see how to make a ring?" He closed his hands on a firefly. He pinched off the yellow light then smeared his ring finger with the bug's soft body.

I took the bug I'd caught and did the same. A band of gold glowed on my finger.

"I know about your daddy," he said. He looked up the hill to the adults, now hidden in dark and covered in smoke, where his mother no doubt was fixing his hotdog for him.

"He died in the war." I held my ringed hand up to my face and spread my fingers so I could pretend I was peering through bars in a jail.

"He was a drunk and he suicided." Mark stared at me. I closed my fingers so that they screened my face from him.

"Big deal." I ran up the hill where the lights shone on my mother, pretty in her skirt and sandals, smelling now of hamburger grease. My yellow ring smeared on my mother's soft skirt as I pressed my head against her warm legs. Mark was behind me and opened his arms to his mother, who swung him around. They laughed that special laugh parent and child often share when the child is still young, the sound of a joyful secret kept between them.

"Mark's a nice boy, isn't he?" my mother said to the air. Then she hummed a song, low and smooth, that I pretended was for me.

In my room that night I asked my mother. "What does 'suicided' mean?"

My back was to her as she brushed my hair. She stopped brushing for a few seconds, then resumed the long, slow strokes.

"Where did you hear that word, honey?"

"Mark. He said Daddy was a drunk and he suicided." I wanted her to hate Mark.

My mother dropped the brush and took my hand. We went to her bedroom where she slid open her closet door. She took out a dark jacket and pants with shiny buttons and a navy wool coat, both covered in clear

5

bags.

"See this?" she said. "This was your father's uniform. He was a soldier in Vietnam. He fought very hard. And this coat was his father's, your grandfather. From the Korean War. Your father wore it all the time. All he wanted to do was make his own father proud. That is what you tell Mark and anyone else who says those terrible things."

She led me back to my bedroom and resumed brushing my hair.

"See these walls?" she said. "Your father painted them. For you. He knew your eyes would be blue before you were even born. Remember that." Then she tucked me in and kissed me goodnight. I fell asleep to my mother playing the piano, the music soft and prayerful.

The lie: Second grade was the year I didn't wear green on St. Patrick's Day because my mother, up early to practice a song for Sunday's service, told me to wear the blue gingham dress she had sewn last summer. Green was not our world. As soon as I took off my coat at school, some of the meaner boys pinched my arms and teased me for forgetting. I ran behind the coat closet and cried into wool coats that smelled like mothballs. The girls in my class formed a circle around me, so I could cry in comfort. One of them, I'm pretty sure it was Carol, gave me a piece of green paper to pin on my dress.

Miss Thompson poked her head into our group. "Come out, Elise. I won't let anyone else pinch you. Here, sit on my lap." She had a chair in the middle of the room, and I climbed onto her pillowy legs and sunk my limbs into her breasts and stomach.

"My daddy died in the war," I said, crying on my

teacher's shoulder.

"My poor dear," Miss Thompson said. She patted my back. "My poor, poor dear."

The class crowded around. "Poor dear," the girls echoed in the same pitying voice as Miss Thompson. From the corner of my eye, I saw Mark, his legs crossed and solemn like the Indians we had studied. I waited for him to tell the class that my daddy was a drunk suicide, and then I would tell everyone how I beat him in a race. Instead, he sat with the other boys who watched me, silent, and I saw for the first time how beautiful he was.

My mother kept a few photos of my father in her bedroom that I would study when she was not around. There was one of him, young and wild-haired in the pea coat from my mother's closet, standing in a foot of snow. Another one was of the two of them before he left for the war, before I was even a promise. In that one I barely recognized my mother. Her hair was styled and curled at the shoulders. She wore a fitted dress and lipstick and was laughing into the camera. My father was behind her, shadowed, his hands wrapped around her waist.

My favorite photo must have been taken not long before he left for good. In it, he was lifting me in the air, an offering to something or someone outside the picture's borders. My mouth, widened in amazement and laughter, mirrored his. He wore a short-sleeved, white button-down shirt. He could have been anyone's dad. A black and white dad, like the ones on the old TV programs. A dad who had just come home from work, with his cropped hair and thin face. A dad who worked hard for his family, who loved us more than anything.

There weren't any pictures of the three of us together,

so I had to imagine it. Me, the baby in his arms. My mother's hand on his shoulder, her hair long and loose. I wondered how he could leave us when he had a baby like me to toss in the air at home, when he had all that he ever needed in that imaginary photo: the three of us that moment perfect, out of time and pain and dread of all that was to come, and that is when I first thought that things were beautiful because they were fleeting and just out of our grasp.

The bracelet: In the fourth grade, like all the other girls, I was in love with Mark. He had wavy brown hair, tan skin, and earth-colored eyes lined with thick, dark lashes. His cheeks were perpetually flushed with a deep rose that warmed his face. After he spoke, he had a habit of lowering his eyes, so that his lashes seemed to darken and curl under the weight of his shuttered lids. His jokes were quiet and his smiles effortless. He had lots of friends, could draw life-like houses and people without effort, and now was the fastest runner in our class. Yet, I wasn't jealous. That would have been like being jealous of the stars or the moon.

It was Carol I was jealous of. Her brother, a grade ahead of us, was good friends with Mark. Carol was not too smart but was the prettiest girl in our class, with honey hair and tiger eyes. She could do the splits and three backhand springs in a row. One day she came to class wearing a bracelet with blue stones that Mark had given her for her birthday. All of us girls admired the sparkles as she twisted her wrist under the fluorescent lights. Don't they look like twinkling stars, Carol said, and we cooed in agreement.

At recess one day, the girls gathered around the metal parallel bars. Carol had removed her skirt so that she could twirl freely in her white bodysuit. The gold and blue bracelet jangled against the metal bar when she spun around, her legs taut and brazenly bare under the spring sun. I walked away from her and toward the baseball field, down the hill to where the boys were choosing kickball teams. There were just two boys left, the fat boy and the new boy. Mark, the captain, picked the new boy and left the fat boy for the other team. While the girls cheered Carol, the fat boy lumbered into the right outfield of no man's land, a place where he would not be noticed. I sat on the hill and watched him pretend to disappear.

After school I would sit on the steps outside our house and listen to my mother play the piano, the chords heavy, her voice loudly singing the praises of God and his infinite love. When I walked in the door, she would stop suddenly, and a look would flicker across her eyes before she got up and made me a snack. For years that look remained unnamed and unknowable, until I myself felt it toward her, the look of the interrupted and put-upon.

The beautiful boy: Although there were more than seven-hundred kids in our eighth grade class, everyone knew who the popular ones were. Sometimes I would spy Carol with those girls. They laughed through lip-glossed teeth, set their alarms for before the sun came up to wash and dry their hair so that it flipped back like Farrah Fawcett's and wore Mia's and Jellies a year before the rest of us. The most popular boy was Mark. He had somehow missed the prepubescent awkwardness that afflicted the other boys—his skin shone olive smooth and pimple free, his eyes were forever rimmed with those dark lashes, the permanent blush still flushed on his cheeks. Between classes he would pull an oversize plastic comb out of his pocket and quickly run the teeth through his hair until the sides softly feathered back like a bird's wing. All the girls in junior high had a crush on him, but by the eighth grade Mark was dating cheerleaders on the freshman squad.

English was my best subject. Mark was in that class and he sat with the other popular boy in the back. I made my new best friend there—Denise—and with her we befriended Brad and Jim, my first guy friends. We sat together, the smartest kids in the class, and as a group we became bold. We wrote double-entendre haikus and sexually explicit sonnets. We answered the questions correctly when called on but never volunteered the answers. I remember the day Brad started to like me. We had been reading Hawthorne's "The Birthmark." Our teacher called on me.

"Hawthorne says that there is nothing more tragic than the death of a beautiful woman. Do you agree with that, Elise?"

I paused. "Actually, there's nothing more tragic than the death of a beautiful man."

The class laughed. Our teacher shook her head. Brad's eyes were on me and his mouth turned in a sly grin.

That afternoon Denise followed me to my locker and whispered in a low voice. "Brad likes you. He says you have nice tits for an eighth grader." She ran her hand over the metal door. "Do you like him?"

I spun the combination of my locker like it was my own wheel of fortune. "I guess so."

"Okay if I tell him?" Denise jerked the metal handle.

"Sure." I bent down to grab my books. My cheeks

were hot. I wondered how large my breasts would grow, and if I should let Brad touch them.

When I rose back up, Denise was staring past my head to the end of the row where Mark stood at his locker. He removed the plastic, wide-tooth comb out of his painter's pants side pocket then ran it through his hair. He followed each comb-through with a pat of his hand, then slid the comb back in its pocket.

"God, he's so good looking. He doesn't act stuck-up either."

"He's always been that way."

"You know him?" Denise touched my shoulder.

"We went to the same elementary school. His parents go to my church." I wanted to tell her about the races and the gold rings. But they would sound silly, so I didn't. "You know Carol Mason? He gave her a bracelet in the fourth grade."

Denise leaned against the locker next to mine and rested her cheek on the cold metal. "Lucky girl. It almost hurts to look at him. He's perfect."

"Yeah." I slammed my locker door. "But he can't be perfect forever."

Brad and I were together for about a month. Sometimes when we giggled and passed notes in English class I would glance at Mark in the back. I wanted him to see that I, Elise, the girl with the dead drunk dad, had a boyfriend, but he never looked my way.

One day toward the end of the school year, I remained in the English classroom to finish reading a note Brad had passed me. I read the part again about how cute I was, and refolded the note into a neat square before settling it in my back pocket. As I gathered my books, I saw Mark holding his English textbook in his right hand, walking toward the door in his button-down shirt and Levi's. He nodded. Having a boyfriend who wrote me sweet notes must have given me the courage to speak.

"Remember that race in kindergarten?"

"What?" He stared at me, his face a question mark, not unkind.

"Nothing." I brushed past him, my face burning.

In eighth grade, my mother went from part to full time at the music store. My afternoons were free then to search for more clues to my father's life. I found his letters underneath her stockings in her lingerie drawer. First was the official letter, that my father was a hero, the only one on his patrol boat to survive a massacre by the North Vietnamese. Soon after that he came home, and a year later in 1972 I was born. Then, when I was a year old, he left again. There were the letters from distant relatives on my father's side. No, they had not seen him, they knew nothing of his disappearance. Then came the letter postmarked from Bangkok dated June 1977. The letter was written in broken English, with no return address or signature. That letter said my father had found love and a good life, but that one night after drinking too much he forgot his happiness and drowned himself in the Kwai River near their village.

The enclosed photo showed my father with thick hair that tipped his shoulders and was tamed with a bandana. Behind him stood a thatched hut and a cluster of bamboo trees. His smile was slack and lopsided; his eyes were small slits from squinting into the sun. He held a bottle of liquor in a toast to the camera. Someone had cut the photo in half.

I touched the razored edge of the photo, wondering

who had cut it. I thumbed my father's face, traced the outline of his hair. The phone rang, and I slid the shoe box back in the dark where I had found it.

After that, my mother's imperfections were clearer to me: her face, flat and furrowed without makeup; her pathetic flowered skirts, the hem unfashionably grazing her lower calves; her shapeless long hair and the strands of gray that she didn't bother hiding.

Over the years at dinner, as we ate our canned peas and chicken casserole, my mother would say things like, "So Mark is in your class again this year." Or "Mark's mother tells me he's bringing home beautiful drawings from art class." Or "That Mark is turning into a handsome young man, and so well-mannered too." By eighth grade though, I'd had enough.

"How's Mark doing in your English class?" she asked one evening as she twirled spaghetti on her fork.

"There's sauce on your chin," I said.

She took her napkin and dabbed the spot under her lower lip.

"Honestly, Mom, can't you try harder? Couldn't you have tried harder?"

She crumpled her napkin and tossed it on the table. "It has nothing to do with trying." She looked like a drooping flower. "Some things are in God's hands."

"Well, then," I said, tossing my own napkin before I stood up. "God, like you, must not give a shit."

The last time: The summer after eighth grade stretched out long and lonely. I thought about English class, how smart and witty I had been, with a boyfriend and everything. Denise and Brad were going together now, so I had no one to hang out with. Sometimes I saw Carol at the neighborhood pool, oiled and brown in her bikini, and she was nice enough to say hi to me although she never asked me to join her and her friends. One afternoon in July, my mother came home early from her job at the music store to tell me Mark had been hit by a truck while riding his bike on his way to his girlfriend's house. Killed instantly. Then she went directly to church to prepare for the funeral service.

Denise called me that night, crying.

"The whole thing is so surreal. I heard he was high and that's why he got run over. They say his body's so messed up they'll have to cremate it. That beautiful, perfect body. I wonder if he was doing it with that cheerleader girlfriend. God, I can't believe it."

"Me neither," I said over her sobs. But I did believe it. I believed in the magic of willing, that I had willed him to die because I needed him to, that I needed him to be forever beautiful and time soon would have changed that, and he wouldn't have been that perfectly shaped receptacle for all that burned within me.

At the funeral I sat in the back. Mark's parents, shrunken, were slumped in the front pew. In a few months they would move to Arizona, where it was hot and sunny and dry all the time. In the choir loft my mother played the organ with appropriate sadness and intensity. All the popular kids crammed in the front. I had never heard such wailing, never seen the church so crowded. Denise and Brad were squeezed in the middle pews, not even bothering to save a space for me. During the cheerleader girlfriend's tearful speech about the tragedy of a life with such promise cut short, I snuck outside and walked over to the hill where Mark and I had raced in kindergarten. A wisp of smoke rose from a figure hidden in the grass. I eased down the hill and lay beside Carol where the sky was open to us.

"Fucking bullshit. Just fucking bullshit." She lifted a joint to her puffed, blotchy face, breathed in, and then held the smoke for a few seconds before exhaling. She offered me the joint. My first. I held the smoke in my mouth for as long as I could.

It would be years before I could look at the pictures of him or my father and see them as merely reflections of myself. It would be years before Mark stopped visiting me in my dreams, his hand outstretched in forgiveness.

I was hoping the joint would help me feel big things, but instead I still only felt small ones. I imagined fireflies flying in front of me, except these ones were uncatchable and their light was blue. "You still got that bracelet?" I asked her.

"What?"

"The one Mark gave you in the fourth grade."

"Shit. I hadn't thought of that thing in years." She took the joint back. "I don't know what happened to it."

I stared at the cloudless sky, the color of my blue fireflies. "I beat him in a race once. We were in kindergarten."

"Big deal." Carol turned her head. "Big fucking deal."

I propped up on my elbows and looked back toward the church. I heard notes of loss and regret along with acceptance of God's will. Then the music stopped, and in that space I saw the church doors swing open, and my mother, in her black robe and stockinged feet, emerged wild-eyed and grief-stricken.

"Elise?" she said in a voice I could barely hear from where I was. "Where are you?"

I hesitated. But she stayed at the threshold of the

church and would not go back in. Finally, I waved to her from the hill.

My mother smiled and waved back, like I was leaving for a long journey. Then she turned and disappeared, a black moment lost under the harsh glare of the sun.

THE REST
OF THE STORY

In June, the morning air is still fresh and smells like cut grass through the car window, which Elise has rolled halfway down. It is Friday, two weeks after Elise's high school graduation. She and her mother drive past their neighbor Philip, the almost-thirty-year-old son of the Sherman's, mowing the lawn. His parents, tired of Northern Virginia suburban living, retired to Florida a year ago and left the house for him. Wearing a T-shirt, cutoffs, and flip-flops, Philip nods in their direction but keeps both hands on the push mower.

"He would be handsome if he cut his hair," Elise's mother says.

"Looks fine the way it is." Elise cranks the window the rest of the way down as her mother punches the radio station button for Paul Harvey's news and information. Three years ago Elise made out with Philip at Carol's brother's high school graduation party. He was the oldest person there and Elise one of the youngest. He was drunk enough to not even recognize her, while she was drunk enough to think he looked like Jim Morrison. They made out on the couch for half an hour before he passed out, prone, mid-kiss. Even drunk he had been a good kisser, slow and sweet, like he had all the time in the world.

Better than Josh, who uses too much tongue too quickly, Elise thinks. She's been playing the good girl with him; he probably thinks she's still a virgin, and she hasn't discouraged him from that notion. She enjoys his company in a comfortable Friday-night-date kind of way, but he doesn't, as Jim Morrison would say, light her fire.

Elise drives through the subdivision five miles above the speed limit—as fast as she can with her mother in the car. The houses, once compact and optimistic, are now, twenty years later, cramped and disappointing. The porches are gradually accumulating broken TV's and unused tire swings. The children who used to play kickball in the streets and hide-and-seek in the yards are grown up, and no one has replaced them. In a few months Elise will also leave for her freshman year in college. Even though home will be only a three-hour drive away, she doesn't plan on visiting much.

She imagines herself in her dorm room, free of her mother's music, alone, playing her father's old albums—Hank Williams, Johnny Cash, George Jones, Tammy Wynette. Grooved between the scratches and pops of the albums are the drunken laments of those lonely and left behind. When she's not alone, she'll listen to her other favorites, Dylan, The Rolling Stones, The Beatles, The Who, The Doors, and of course the music of her time: U2, REM, INXS, The B-52s. But the old country stuff, that will be just her and her record player.

"Good Morning Americans," Paul Harvey booms from the radio. As he launches into that day's Rest of the Story, her mother leans forward and holds her hand up, shushing an already quiet car. Elise reminds herself that once she's in college she won't have to listen to Paul Harvey ever again.

So far this week Paul Harvey has told listeners about a Jew named Heinz who escaped Bavaria and changed his named to…Henry Kissinger; Catherine Campbell who unsuccessfully auditioned to become Scarlett O'Hara and was the mother of…Patricia Hearst; "Bab," the baby kidnapped in Italy in 1839 who was…Gilbert of Gilbert and Sullivan; and Horatio Alger, known as the American success story, who actually died…broke. Today's story is about the composer Wagner who had a secret collaborator and critic who was…Peps, Wagner's dog.

"Well, I'll be." Her mother chuckles as she places a brown paper bag, the top neatly folded, next to Elise's leg. "Leftover roast beef on cracked wheat. Remember to bring the bag back."

Elise nods, but knows she probably won't. She always tries, but by lunchtime the bottom of the bag is soggy, torn, unusable. Whenever Elise picks her mother up from work, the saved lunch bag, creased into the size of an envelope, pokes out from her mother's macramé handbag, ready for re-use.

They are on the highway now; four lanes are no longer enough to hold the morning traffic, which jerks to stops and starts every few minutes. On both sides of the highway trees are falling to make way for bigger, newer houses with wide windows and high ceilings. The construction workers have been up for hours. Sunburned and broad-shouldered, they guzzle soft drinks straight from the bottle. Elise is certain they are squinting not at the gleam of metal and glass from the highway but at her, with powerful but disconcerting x-ray vision. Elise rolls her window up to keep the dust out.

"Houses sure go up fast these days. I expect they'll be done by the end of the summer." Her mother punches the button programmed to her favorite classical music station. When Bach comes on, she tilts her head back and closes her eyes. Her hands flutter and her singing increases in conviction and clarity. "A mighty fortress is our God, a trusty shield and weapon; he helps us free from every need, that hath us now o'ertaken."

Elise transports herself back to her fantasy dorm room. In this scenario, Josh conveniently doesn't exist, and instead she is listening to Johnny Cash's "Ring of Fire" while making out with a shirtless boy named Dylan or Jude who wears faded Levi's torn at one knee and walks to class barefoot.

Traffic eases up past the construction, and Elise rolls her window down again for some fresh air, but only breathes in the exhaust from the cars in front of her. She exits off the highway and pulls into an aging strip mall where she drops her mother off at twenty past eight in front of Brown's Music.

"Glad I'm early today. This new manager, Mr. Wisneski, is a real stickler for time." Her mother holds her purse and lunch in one hand and raises her floral cotton skirt above her knees with the other as she steps out of the car.

Elise exits the lot and punches the button for the classic rock station. The Who's "My Generation" is on. She turns up the volume and sings along.

Elise's summer job is a receptionist-slash-assistant at a company that does consulting work for the Federal Government, the nature of which she doesn't understand but senses is somehow related to purchasing. She scribbles messages on a yellow "While You Were Out" pad, puts calls through with the push of a button, and word processes the occasional memo or purchase order that lands on her desk. The first fifteen minutes of the morning are always busy as Elise deals with those calling in sick and covers for the others who are late. She dispenses messages like prescriptions as the employees straggle in, more or less on time.

This morning, Ken, the manager, shows up last, wearing a short-sleeve white oxford and navy chinos. Ten minutes later he brings Elise coffee for her to make from his personal stash—French roast. Ever since he lived in France for a year after college, he tells her, he can't drink "that Maxwell House shit." It's the only time she's heard him swear. He's not bad looking for someone in his late thirties, she thinks, tall and slim with curly dark hair and brown eyes. The phone rings.

"It's your wife." Elise tries to meet Ken's eyes, but he's staring at her paisley shirt.

"I think you missed a button," he says.

Elise glimpses the white bra at the base of her cleavage and buttons her shirt up to right below her collarbone.

"Thanks," she mumbles, feeling red and sweaty. Ken nods and strides to his office.

A few hours later, Elise goes to Ken's office to return the worn copies of Carl Jung's *Modern Man In Search of A Soul* and Sigmund Freud's *Interpretation of Dreams* he has loaned her. She has been reading them during the slow hours and on her lunch break, scribbling notes on blank Post-Its as she reads.

"Still want to be a psychology major?" Ken looks preppy but in a casual-not-too-uptight way, Elise has decided. He gestures toward the empty chair across from his desk. She sits on its edge and crosses her legs.

"I think so. Freud, though, seems outdated to me," she says.

"How so?" He is leaning back in his chair, grinning, hands cupped behind his head.

"I just don't see how everything can be about sex." She crosses her bare legs, glances down at her open-toed kitten heels.

Ken laughs. She always feels he is in on a joke she is too naive to understand. He flips through the Jung, quickly finding the passage he wants. "Remember this? 'The great decisions of human life have as a rule far more to do with the instincts and other mysterious unconscious factors than with conscious will and well-meaning reasonableness.'"

"What about it?" Elise had written that exact phrase on one of her Post-It notes and tucked it under the computer keyboard for quick reference.

"We can discuss it more over lunch," Ken says.

"If you're not busy." Elise stands, suddenly aware of how cold his office is, of the goose bumps on her legs and her nipples visible through her blouse.

"I know a place down the street. Be ready at noon."

She feels his eyes hot on her back as she reaches for the door. She tells herself she can stop this anytime she wants.

♌

Lunch is in a diner that no one from work would go to. They both order hamburgers and Elise asks him about his college days.

"It was a great time," Ken says. "Lots of crazy stuff back then."

"Did you drop acid?"

"Sure. Why do you ask?" Ken pushes his plate away and signals the waitress for a coffee.

"Just curious." She dips a French fry in ketchup then washes down the greasy sweetness with her Coke. Blood, she remembers a babysitter telling her a long time ago, tastes like ketchup.

"You're curious about a lot of things. What else do you want to know?" He takes out a pack of cigarettes, Gauloises, and lights one.

"Your wife. Your marriage."

"She knows I'm not happy. But she's very dependent. Depressed. I'm trying to get her back on her feet. Then I'm leaving her." The lines sound tired to Elise, like he's said them to himself—or other women—for a long time.

"Kids?"

"Two boys." He crushes the cigarette in the plastic ashtray and smoothes the napkin in front of him. "I love them to death, but I hadn't planned on them. She wanted them. I thought they would make her happy." He calls the waitress over for the check. He raises his eyes and reaches for Elise's hand. "I've never done this before. I swear."

She squeezes his hand, like they are closing a business deal. Unlike her fantasies about college life, this fantasy is not her own.

After she gets off work, Elise parks in front of Brown's Music and air guitars to "Layla," a song in heavy rotation on the classic radio station. Her mother waves and scurries to the car, as if she is late for an appointment. After she fastens her seatbelt, she stretches her legs and fans them with the hem of her skirt. Elise rotates the dial to the local news station for the traffic report. They only have five miles on the highway between Brown's Music and home, but if there is an accident it can take a half hour to drive that small stretch of road. Today, the traffic is light.

While she drives, Elise steals glimpses of her mother, eyes closed, purse slack on her stomach, one hand on her chest, the other smoothing her skirt. She doesn't look tired so much as elsewhere. She opens her eyes suddenly as if she's been awakened from a dream.

"Where's your lunch?"

"In the fridge at work. I ate out. I'll have it on Monday." Elise glances at her mother's lap, both hands now clasping the braided handles of the macramé purse. "Where's yours?"

She covers her mouth with her hand. "Guess I didn't eat mine either." She clears her throat. "What are you and Josh doing tonight?"

"The same."

"They say the first year of college is the hardest. Lucky that Josh can show you the ropes."

They pass by the place where the housing division is being built. The construction workers are gone for the day although the sun won't set for a few more hours. Her mother taps the window.

"Look at that. They put the doors and windows in today."

The car in front of them stops suddenly, and Elise slams the brakes. A cacophony of car horns breaks out. Then the car in front starts again.

"How's business?" Elise asks, keeping both hands on the wheel.

"Jack says that we need to push more of that rock stuff. Says church music is not selling well these days." Her mother sniffs.

"Jack?"

"That's what he wants us to call him. New management style, I guess." She smoothes her skirt and returns to clutching the macramé purse. "He's a gentleman though, through and through. I'll give him that."

"A gentleman and a scholar I'm sure," Elise says. She thinks of Ken then, and the kiss they shared after lunch, an expert kiss, and his expert hands running down the nape of her neck to the small of her back.

They drive by the Sherman's yard. Philip is reclining in a lounge chair on the freshly cut lawn with a glass in his hand. He waves as they drive by.

"Mom, don't wave back."

"Why not?"

"Once a bad egg always a bad egg, don't you think?" Elise is thinking of Philip's lips, how they were all over her face and neck, and the slight stubble on his face that scratched her and turned her on at the same time.

"That's not what God says."

Elise tilts her head upward.

"Well God, I guess I can do whatever I want, huh?"

"Elise honey, don't be glib."

Elise smiles and thinks of the phone call she will make to Ken in a few hours.

That evening Elise's mother knocks on her bedroom door telling her Josh has arrived. Prompt as usual. Squeezing the phone between her neck and shoulder while she twirls her hair, Elise tells Ken that she has to go and promises to wear a shorter skirt on Monday.

She pushes herself up from her bed so she faces the mirror. Her cheeks are flushed and her hair is sticking to her neck. She runs pink lipgloss across her lips and smoothes her hair into a ponytail. As she walks down the darkened hall toward the living room, she sees her mother setting a glass of tea down in front of Josh on the couch.

"Lots of lemon and sugar, the way you like it."

"Thank you, ma'am." Josh leans forward to take the drink.

"Oh, and could you remind your mother that we're meeting a half hour before the first service to go over the Bach song?"

"I'll be sure to do that."

Josh, wearing tan shorts and a navy Polo shirt, stands up as Elise approaches him. He holds the glass out to her, and she gulps a third of the tea before she returns it. He brings the rim, now smudged with her pink gloss, to his lips. He drains the rest of the tea and crunches the remaining ice cubes. Her mother takes the empty glass back to the kitchen.

"You look great," he whispers. Beneath the bite of his cologne she smells a breath mint, and under that the sour smell of beer. She smiles and squeezes his hand.

"We're going now," Elise calls.

"Honey, can you come here for a minute?"

In the kitchen her mother turns from the sink and wipes her hands on a dish towel. She tucks a few loose hairs behind Elise's ear then places her hands, still damp, on Elise's shoulders.

"Josh's parents are some of my best singers." She pauses. "I hope you won't hurt him."

"Mom." Elise steps back so that her mother is no longer touching her.

"Okay. Okay." Her mother's hands are suspended in mid air, as if she is about to start a song with the choir at church. She turns and plunges them into the soapy water in the sink.

"I'll be home by midnight."

"You can stay out later you know."

"I know."

Her mother nods and continues washing the glasses.

On the way to one of the chain restaurants at the mall, they split a can of Bud from the twelve-pack in the cooler in the back seat. After dinner they walk to the Cineplex at the other end of the mall. Elise suggests *Wild at Heart* and Josh agrees, she can tell, just to please her. In the darkened theater, Josh alternates between putting his arm around her and taking sips from the beer they've smuggled in Elise's purse. While the two main characters, Sailor and Lula, have sex, Elise thinks of the fate of all the boys in her life so far. The one she lost her virginity to last summer, he is now in college somewhere in the Midwest; the first one who told her he loved her now has a Mohawk and wears a spiked collar; the boy who insisted on saving her from drowning when she was fourteen—a snake had fallen into the boat and she'd jumped into the lake—he's been accepted at MIT; her first boyfriend, the one from the eighth grade, now looks through her in the halls at school; Mark, the beautiful one, had died at thirteen never knowing; her father of course, also dead, didn't give her a chance. And Ken, with his Gauloises and French roasted coffee, probably watching TV with his wife this very moment, although they'd be sitting in separate chairs, his fate is still unknown.

Afterward, in the parked car in the driveway to Elise's house, they drink a few more beers and discuss the movie. Josh tells her he hated it—he liked *Twin Peaks,* but this one was too dark and disturbing, and besides, it demeans women. She agrees, telling him she is repulsed by Willem Dafoe's character, Bobby Peru, when he tries to seduce Lula in the hotel room, telling her, "Say 'fuck me' soft—then I'll leave." That's what she tells Josh, but secretly she is turned on and plays the scene over and over in her mind, imagining Ken saying it to her in a seedy hotel room down the street from the office.

Ten minutes before midnight Elise tells him she must go in, and Josh walks her to the door. With one hand on the doorknob, she turns to face him.

Elise sees "that look," his eyes fixed and wanting. He puts his hand behind her neck and draws her toward him. She breathes in Josh's dime-store cologne still strong on his neck and collar. He thrusts his tongue, cold from the beer, in her slack mouth. She lets him keep his tongue in there, flailing about like a fish out of water. She thinks of Paul Harvey's story about The Code of Love drafted by a group of hard core feminists, "Love cannot extend itself into marriage. A resisting lover is always more desirable. Whoever cannot keep a secret cannot love. Those who are prone to love are equally prone to fear." Then, the rest of the story: The Code of Love was written in 1174.

Elise pulls away and gives Josh a final quick kiss.

"Good night." She turns the doorknob.

He steps backs and shoves his hands in his pockets. "Night. I'll call you later this week."

She pecks him on the cheek then closes the door and turns off the porch light as soon as he's out of the driveway.

By July the air is sticky with late-blooming honeysuckles. Friday on their way to work, they see Phillip mowing the lawn. Even though it is the coolest time of the day his skin shimmers under the sun. He waves.

"Why do you have to wave at him? You look ridiculous." Elise tries to hide the irritation in her voice.

"He's a good neighbor. He's nice."

"Doesn't take much from a man to please you." Elise wipes the sweat off her lips, decides to change the subject so she can skate over her own meanness. "I think we have the only car in the world without air conditioning."

"Couldn't afford any options." Her mother sticks her hand out the open window and spreads her fingers against the wind.

Elise shifts her legs. "I'm already sticking to the seat."

"You'll dry off once you get inside." Her mother's hair is coiled in a bun. Gray wisps stick to her neck. She turns on the radio to Paul Harvey then puts the lunch bag beside Elise. "BLT, your favorite."

Elise glances at the bag, and then brakes for the congestion ahead. Yesterday there had been an accident and they didn't move for thirty minutes. The construction workers, now tanned and muscular, put the siding up last week. She thinks she sees one winking at her, but she can't tell if it's that or just sun in his eyes.

"I told you I'm eating out these days," Elise says.

"You're not going to have any money for school."

"I'm saving, don't worry. Anyway, I'm sure your boss—Jack—will like the lunch. He always does."

"Someone has to eat it." Her mother shrugs, reclaims the lunch bag, nestles it in her lap. "Are you sure that skirt isn't too short for work?"

"Mom. I've told you."

"I'll be quiet." Her mother touches her finger to her mouth.

"Meet Mary Louise." Paul Harvey talks about Mary Louise's simple childhood, then her three marriages, then her call to New York. "Soon she became the woman you know…the bright tough roustabout of stage and silent screen…Mary Louise Cecilia… 'Texas Guinan.'" Paul Harvey speaks of her fame and a reporter, Lowell Thomas, who remembered her from when he was a boy infatuated with her. "For the little girl from Waco who rode the rodeo shows to New York City…the brash blonde who bombarded the Big Apple, belting ballads from a swinging basket…the speakeasy mistress of ceremonies who blazed a brazen trail across the Prohibition Era…'Texas Guinan'…Lowell Thomas remembers as his…school teacher. His Sunday school teacher! And now you know the rest of the story."

Her mother smiles and turns to the classical music station. She hums along to a Mozart symphony playing on the radio.

"You know, Jack was telling me that people play Mozart to help children with speech problems. Isn't that fascinating?"

"Sure is." Elise brakes in front of Brown's Music. Scotch-taped to the windows are outdated Beatles and Boston posters that frame an electric guitar resting in the display case.

Her mother pulls down the visor mirror and runs coral lipstick over her lips then blots them with a tissue. "For the customers."

"Okay, Mom. Have a good day."

"You too." After her mother disappears into the store, Elise plays with the dial. She's in the mood for some of the old country classics, but instead of Johnny or Hank or Willie or Patsy she only finds new songs by people whose names she doesn't even know. "No soul," she whispers, and punches in the classic rock station, waiting for the commercials to pass.

Noon. Elise's eyes are closed. There's nothing at this moment but his moist kisses on her neck, collarbone, the damp spot between her breasts. Her bra (the good white one) is unhooked, his hand is cruising down her body, her legs (did she shave this morning?), to the white lace underwear (he has a thing for white), tugged down, nothing but his lips on her kneecaps, feathery on the insides of her thighs, you're so wet he whispers, so clean and innocent, but she doesn't feel innocent, she feels like she's sucked into a tunnel where pleasure exists in a black spot independent of the world outside these doors, a dark place where nothing can touch her except this feeling she's being pulled in, and she makes too much noise and doesn't open her eyes until she comes. Then he puts the condom on and fucks her on his desk.

Afterward, they smoke Ken's Gauloises.

"We should go to a hotel next time," Ken says. "This is too dangerous."

"Fine by me." She points to one of the framed posters in his office. "I like that."

"Picasso," Ken says. "From his Blue period." He wraps his arms around her. "Ah, if only I could take you away from here, I would teach you so much."

"Where would you take me?"

"Another country," he says. "That's where real life is."

"My dad thought the same, I guess," Elise says. She holds his arms and is relieved when he doesn't ask her to explain because he is too occupied with the tunnels in her ears and the tiny hairs on her neck.

While she waits for her mother in front of Brown's Music, Elise twirls through the radio stations but can't find anything. She jerks the key out of the steering wheel and opens the car door just as her mother rushes out, her coral mouth shaped in a soft O.

Clouds fatten the sky and the air has cooled slightly, a sure sign of rain. The windows are rolled down in most of the other cars, the air conditioner defiantly turned off. Elise and her mother don't turn the radio on, deciding not to compete with the chaos of music from the surrounding cars. She looks at the swollen sky and hopes the weather will clear by Monday, as the drive is much duller if the construction workers aren't there. She's come to measure their progress as hers—she's counting on them to be done with the first few houses by summer's end.

As they drive by the Sherman's, Philip waves to them. He's on the porch, a full glass in his hand, reading a book. Her mother waves back. Elise pretends not to notice.

Elise waits until 7:50 before she calls him. He told her he would call at 7:30. He's been late before, but Josh is coming soon. His wife's pottery class is on Monday, Wednesdays, and Fridays, and that is when they usually talk on the phone. She dials his number by touch. A woman answers, her voice throaty and animated, not frail or crazy-sounding in the least. Elise hangs up, her hands shaking.

Josh stands from the couch with his glass as Elise

walks in the living room. She is wearing jeans and a T-shirt and no makeup. Her eyes are red and puffy. He raises his iced tea to her. She takes a long drink and thanks him. Josh nods and says goodbye to her mother, who's at the piano practicing a song for Sunday's service. She wishes them a good time before they are out the door.

That night they watch *Pretty Woman*. Elise says in this world prostitutes don't get a millionaire Richard Gere as a boyfriend, while Josh says Julia Roberts is unbelievable as a whore because her skin is too clear. After they finish what remains of the twelve-pack in his car, Elise asks Josh in for the first time. On the couch, she reclines, inviting his body to lie on top of hers. This time her tongue is in his mouth, and she lets him touch her breasts and rub her crotch through her jeans. She waits for the feelings to show up. He rocks on top of her but she remains motionless, her fingers spread like a web on his back. He's not wearing the cologne tonight, and she can taste the beer beading through his pores. He smells like Philip on that night four years ago, but Philip's mouth and hands were slow and heavy, like they were under water. Finally, Elise gives up and tells Josh she's tired. He pulls her closer to her.

"You weren't tired a few minutes ago." His words sound sloppy, foreign, like he has just come from a place where language doesn't exist.

"Josh. Get off me." She sits up so that he must as well.

He opens his mouth and then closes it. He stares at her hard then stands up, brushes his pants, smoothes his shirt.

"All right then," he says, letting out a deep breath. "I'll wait."

She walks him to the door and gives him a quick kiss goodnight before turning out the lights. She stands in the dark and silence, waiting for him to leave so that she can step outside and secretly smoke one of Ken's cigarettes under the summer sky.

By August the air is too heavy to breathe, and the world

smells like gas and melted tar. Most mornings, including this Friday, Elise has to shake herself awake behind the wheel. She hasn't been sleeping well lately.

"Where's Philip?" Her mother asks.

"Must have decided to let the grass grow," Elise says.

"I think it looks all right." Her mother pauses. "Still, I hope he's not sick."

"I'm sure he'll recover."

"You didn't eat breakfast."

Elise turns the radio on and lets Paul Harvey take over for the rest of the ride.

The construction workers look not so much tanned as dirty now. Elise no longer feels that they are staring at her, but instead that they are looking through her to some point that she cannot see.

"Hard to believe there's only two more weeks of work for you," her mother says.

"Yep."

"And then you'll be gone. Off to college." Her mother's voice is light but forced at the same time.

"Hard to believe," Elise manages as she pulls into Brown's.

Her mother slides out of the car, her purse bulging with the lunches she's packed in the two crisp paper bags. The Beatles posters have curled from the humidity, and the electric guitar is spotted with dust. Her mother walks toward the door, which magically opens as if on command. "Blowing in the Wind" is on the radio. Elise scans the stations, searching for something faster and with more of a beat.

As they smoke their Gauloises, Elise looks out Ken's office window, which has a view of the other buildings in the complex. She wonders why they call them office parks, since there is no park to be seen. She's not wearing underwear, at Ken's request, and can feel the wet stickiness between her legs drying in the air conditioned room.

"We never did go to a hotel," she says.

"Too expensive," he replies.

"I want to do acid."

"No can do," Ken says. He backs up from the window and picks up a stack of papers on his desk. "I've got responsibilities now. You'll have to wait a few more weeks until college for that stuff."

"Why? I don't need your permission."

"Of course not," Ken says. He sits in his chair, studies the calendar on his desk. "Of course not."

She stands by the door, waiting for him to say goodbye, but he doesn't. The way he's scrutinizing his calendar says it all: he's forgotten that she's there, that she even exists.

After work Elise drops the butt of her cigarette out her window, and pops in a mint before pulling into one of the empty spaces in front of Brown's Music. Her mother is waiting outside and when she gets in, Elise guesses from the red eyes and puffed skin that she has been crying.

"Are you okay?"

Her mother nods. "Tough day at work. Jack says they may have to close the store."

"You'll lose your job?"

Her mother shakes her head slowly. "It won't come to that. I'll probably be transferred to the main branch in DC."

"That commute?"

"I don't have much choice." Her mother purses her lips then exhales through her nose. "What movie are you seeing tonight with Josh?"

They pass the new subdivision. The houses in the front look finished from the outside.

"Actually, we're going to a party."

"Where?"

"Remember Carol Mason?"

"That girl with that pretty blonde hair and brown eyes from your elementary school? The one who did back handsprings at every school event?"

"Yeah. She's having it."

"I didn't know you were friends."

"It's not that kind of party. Anyone can come."

"It's not one of those drug parties, is it?"

"Mom."

"I'll keep quiet." She touches her finger to her lips.

They listen to the news until they turn the corner by the Sherman's house.

"I really should call and make sure he is okay," her mother says.

"Probably just on vacation."

"The grass needs mowing. I'm worried."

"You can mow it for him," Elise says.

"I don't know if that would be appropriate."

"That was a joke."

"Oh." She presses her lips together, and Elise thinks she might start crying again. "I was just trying to help."

That evening, Josh rings the doorbell, and Elise greets him with an iced tea. She's wearing a pink top with her jeans and has her hair down. Josh tells her she looks great. After dinner at Bennigan's, they drive to Carol's house a few blocks from where Elise lives.

Philip answers the door, and at first seems unable to recognize Elise. His eyes are red and glassy. Then he smiles.

"Elise." He draws out her name, as if he is remembering everything as he says it. "Good to see you." He stares at Josh.

"Philip, Josh. Josh, Philip, my neighbor."

Josh extends his hand and Philip takes it briefly. Josh puts his arm around Elise's shoulder.

"Hey, you must know Carol then," Philip says to Elise. "She's out back. Keg is in the kitchen." He leads them into the house.

"I'll get the beers," Josh says once they are inside. People from Elise's high school, past and present, fill the living room with plastic cups of beer and familiar conversation. She recognizes the new hip band that people are listening to, Nirvana, blaring from the stereo. She is relieved to see none of her old boyfriends are here. Philip lingers.

"You look different," he says.

"How's that?"

"All grown up." He takes out a cigarette and points the pack toward her. She waves her hand. His hair is longer than it was at the beginning of the summer and is now past his shoulders. The living room already reeks of spilt beer and vomit. She wonders how Carol will explain this to her mother when she returns.

"Your lawn needs mowing," she says.

Philip smiles. "I know. I know. I've been slipping." He takes a drag from his cigarette. "Hey, your mom is one sweet lady. Not all stuck-up like you."

Josh returns with two large plastic cups of beer. "Let's go out," he says. Taking Elise by the arm, he guides her through the patio door to the back where people in cutoff shorts, T-shirts, and sandals congregate in fluid yet discrete groups. One of the groups is sitting in a circle on the lawn passing a bong while a bearded man strums Neil Young on his guitar. Elise waves to Carol, who breaks from the circle and runs to her.

"Elise," she slurs. "Long time."

"Since graduation." Elise raises her arm to steady Carol. She's not as pretty as she used to be—she's bonier now and her dirty blond hair is shapeless, limp. "You with Philip?"

"Yeah," Carol giggles. "Sort of. He's hot for an old

guy, don't you think?"

The guitar player shouts, "Carol! Come back and sing for us," and the small circles choruses its approval. She staggers back to the scattered applause of her return.

"That's one messed-up girl," Josh says before gulping half the beer in his cup. His upper lip glistens from the foam.

The circle is singing REM's "The One I Love" now. Carol's voice, a knife dipped in honey, rises above the others: *a simple prop to occupy my time.* Elise wishes Carol would ask her to join them.

"She was really popular in elementary school. She could work those parallel bars like no one else," Elise says.

Josh laughs. "That was a long time ago."

And one day, this too will be a long time ago, Elise thinks as they sit on the ground far from the circle. The pot smoke doesn't reach them. Instead, Elise inhales the cleansing scent of night dew on fresh cut grass.

Five beers later, Josh confesses that he is not returning to college that fall because he did not get the required 2.0 GPA and now he's forced to take a year off. "Too much drinking and not enough studying." He picks up fistfuls of grass then throws them back on the ground.

"Too bad," Elise says, and pats his hand. Secretly, she is relieved that he won't be going to the same college as her, and when she stares at him, chubby-faced, red, a little sad, she knows the charade is over.

She stands up, wobbly, and excuses herself to the bathroom. Down the hall Philip is leaning against the doorway to a bedroom, holding a beer, his eyes half-lidded. He's smiling at her, as if he's been waiting for her all night to come to him. They walk into the empty bedroom and close the door. His kisses are sloppier than she remembers, his hands less controlled. His skin tastes like over-salted fish.

"You got any acid?" she whispers in his ear. He murmurs something she doesn't understand. She nudges his shoulder, and he collapses on the bed.

Through the slice of the bedroom door, she catches Josh waiting in line for the bathroom. He smiles at her at first, but then his forehead and mouth tighten. She feels hot breath on her neck and smells the yeasty sweetness of beer behind her. Philip makes a drunken grab for her, but catches only the air as she stands up and escapes the room. In the hallway she stops in front of Josh, whose hand is raised as if he might slap her.

"I'm tired. Of everything. I'm going home." She stares at his hand, daring him the slap.

"Be my guest." He closes his hand to a fist and shoves it in his pants pocket. "I don't care anymore."

"That's better." She turns from him and walks out the door.

She is only four houses from the party when Josh catches up with her in his car. She shakes her head and continues walking, careful to stay under the street lights.

"Come on, Elise. I don't want your mom mad at me."

She stops and stares at him. "So this is all about my mom?" She's scared now. "You mean I got it all wrong?"

"I don't know what you're talking about. I'm just saying that if your mom tells mine that I didn't treat you right, I'm in bigger trouble than I already am." She sees then that he's scared too. She gets in the car, and he drives her home. After he turns off the engine, Josh leans over and kisses her harder than he ever has. He grabs her shoulders then jerks her shirt up, pushing her against the passenger door. Elise palms his shoulders and pushes him back.

"No more," she says, reaching for the handle. He dives forward again as she opens the door. She tumbles onto the pavement then jumps up as quick as a cat. She has her hands up in front of her chest, ready to box. Shards of gravel stick into her palms, and as she closes her hands tighter, the stones dig deeper.

Josh is splayed across the passenger seat, his hands reaching out to her.

"I know about you," he says slowly. "I know." He moans slightly and his fingers move up and down on the car seat like he's playing an invisible guitar. Then he vomits on the edge of the seat, and the sudden smell of sour beer and musk and men's sweat rises from the car and chokes her. Elise runs into the house. A small balding man with a mustache is sitting on the couch.

"You must be Elise." He stands stiffly.

Her mother emerges from the hall wearing a yellow summer dress. Her coral lipstick is smeared slightly at the top.

"You're home early." She brushes by Elise to the kitchen. "Would you like some iced tea? I was just preparing some for Mr. Wisneski. He's here to discuss ideas for getting more business at the store."

Elise stares at this man—Jack—in his open-collared shirt and polyester pants. He is younger than she has imagined. She hears Josh drive away. She wonders where Jack is parked.

"I think I'll just go to sleep."

Jack Wisneski looks pointedly at his watch and professes to be shocked at the time. He shakes Elise's hand before Elise escapes to her room.

Moment later she falls into bed, trying to convince herself that the last few hours have just been a drunken hallucination, a bad dream she will wake from. Then she hears her mother playing the piano, some church thing again, quiet so as not to disturb her, yet loud enough to score her dreams with purple notes dancing under a darkened sky.

Saturday morning Elise wakes up early, the world too bright, her mouth scraped dry. She shuffles to her window to pull down the shade. Outside the ground and trees look covered in snow. Then she sees her mother midway on a ladder that leans against a tree in their yard. She's teasing out bits of toilet paper stuck in the branches. On the street scrawled in white foot-long letters is: "Elise is a slut." She pulls down the shade and crawls back into bed, convinced that she is still asleep.

When she does wake up later in the afternoon, the trees are no longer bandaged in white. She half-believes that the toilet-papering never happened, but then she catches the small flecks, like dandruff on the grass, and then she makes out the white block letters on the street. She ticks off the reasons her mother hasn't removed the message on the street: it could be she didn't see it, that the street is not her property, or that she wants to make sure Elise sees the message and learns a lesson. Whatever the reason, Elise vows to erase it by morning.

That night, after her mother goes to sleep, Elise sneaks outside and faces the letters glowing on the pavement of the lamp-lit street. Shaking the spray paint can until her arm hurts, she traces the white letters over with the black paint until they blend into the black tar of the road. She paints over "slut" first and starts on her name. She finishes covering the "s" in "Elise" when the headlights come toward her. She dives behind a bush in the Sherman's yard, clutching her can of paint. She re-emerges once the taillights disappear.

"Hey, what are you doing?" Philip stands on the edge of his lawn, but doesn't step onto the road.

"Just painting over something someone wrote."

"It's only soap, it'll wash away the next time it rains," he says. "That paint, though, that will be around a lot longer."

She stops spraying and watches the black seep into the pavement. She wonders if he is the one who did it.

"That stuff used to happen to me all the time," Philip says. He has suddenly reappeared under the streetlight that illuminates his yard. She can see his cut-off shorts, but his feet are hidden under the overgrown grass. His hair is tied back in a ponytail, and he looks like he does in the mornings when he is mowing the lawn. She wonders if he remembers last night.

"Come on over," he says. "I won't bite." He walks to the door and stands.

Behind her are the turned-off lights and shuttered windows of her house. In front of her is Philip, waiting.

"I'm not a slut," she says, walking toward him, holding the spray paint.

"Believe me, I know what a slut is, and baby, that's not you." He takes the paint can, opens the door. His hand is warm and tight in hers as he leads her into the dark strangeness of his house. "There's nothing wrong with a little love every now and then."

She wants to tell him, no, no, I need it a lot more often than that, but instead she holds his hand tight, ready to follow him wherever he'll take her.

Monday, Elise drives over the black and white soap message as they pass by the Sherman's un-mown yard. "Elis slut" is in black paint, "e is a" in white soap. The clouds are dark and the air smells like rain. The college boys are gone from the construction site, replaced by skinny, bearded men who look grateful for a job. Finally, her mother turns on the radio. Paul Harvey is telling the story of Gladys and her second husband, a no-good Norwegian who drives away on his motorcycle when she gets pregnant. Yet, Paul Harvey says, this man, Edward Mortenson, this *uneasy rider*, often wondered what would become of his child he had never met. But Ed would never know the answer because he died from a motorcycle accident and was buried in a pauper's grave. "Although Ed was gone, the trail of broken hearts would lead on and on. Ed's little girl...his daughter by Gladys...would walk it alone...through the heat of camera lights and the cold of white chiffon. She became: Marilyn Monroe."

"Whatever you're doing, be careful," her mother says.

"I could say the same for you."

"It's not what you think," her mother says.

"Exactly." Elise thinks about how after this week she'll never see Ken again, and she's glad for that. She imagines herself in the arms of some college boy. He'll play the songs he wrote on his guitar for her, and she'll sleep over at his place. She'll keep her father's albums under her bed but won't have time to play them.

"I had an uncle once. I know more than you give me credit for." Her mother reaches over and touches Elise's leg briefly, then pulls back. Elise nods but says nothing.

This is the only time her mother will mention the mysterious uncle. Years later, when Elise has the conviction and clarity to ask about the uncle and Jack Wisneski and her father, her mother will no longer be alive to answer.

And in the next moments when her mother leaves the car with one packed lunch, her lips bare and scrubbed clean, Elise will start to change the station, then decide against it, and instead will listen to Paul Harvey saying, "Don't let noisy news distress you. Don't let the headline writers rain on your parade. As Mark Twain once said, 'Wagner's music is better than it sounds.'"

TEMPO

Mother. You were always music. Played the organ at church. I clutched the cold metal of my chair as the music crescendoed. The congregation was drowned out by the booming chords. You nodded toward the choir, fifteen of them, seven men, eight women, as they sang the harmonies of the hallelujah chorus.

Because of your music, you would not know. You would not know the wispy gray fog, always in my periphery, creeping slowly around my ears, ready to turn to smoke. You would not know the muffled sounds, whispers, cold, quiet, soothing, like snow softly begging me to sleep. The white snow and the white closets, heavy and light, rolling into fog that circled my throat. And then I smelled smoke. So I ran.

I won't bore you about how I got here (plane, train, tailwind), but I was here, in San Francisco, that city of ruin, temporal, winding, like the past I never had, a city that at any moment could shake and quake and tumble to the ground.

You would not understand what it meant to want to run, that manic, bright, burning desire to leave by whatever means possible to save your life, to save the voices, and once you are there, there, there, you don't know how or why you did it, only that you no longer care or have the energy to save yourself.

I ran to water, to the ocean, to San Francisco. There in the Castro, I went to one of the gay boy barbers and got my hair cut above my ears, the bangs long.

I will tell you, Mother, that I bought a motorcycle, that my hair was cut short, that I carried a knife tucked into my boot. I tell you this so you know I live in the city, not a town, that I have to protect myself from robbers and rapists, from staring down the barrels of guns, metal pressed against the temple of my head, from being robbed at gunpoint at the library as I step out at two in the afternoon on a Friday into the fog and rain and wind. That I usually can't reach for my knife, but I know it's there, the cool, metal blade against the hot leather of my boot.

The guy at the café. He was not handsome, but he was my type. The openness, the workhorse face. I had talked to him only once, yet I saw my future with him and his rolled-up sleeves and self-assured smiles, passionate, focused, a chef who sliced. The garlic skin, faded jeans, circles under his eyes. His restaurant, a café with freshly ground coffee and sandwiches with vegetables from local farms.

The man was my future. Us. Old, warm, together. I knew it, and because I knew, I waited. Waited for when I was ready for him, to meet him, look him in the eye, and then someday, marry him, someday have a child with tired brown eyes like his. I saw him holding our child, a girl, as she ran up and down the aisle of the café, demanding our attention. I would be their shadow goddess.

He would be a person whose name I'd say over and over, just to hear the sound. Just to calm myself at night.

I avoided him because of this, the timing wasn't right, and I thought he would wait, frozen, unchanged, for years behind the café glass.

I must tell you how happy I was there, how alive

I felt in a city that is grown up. This wind shakes me awake, and I move with a rhythm that makes all of the desperate cries, close calls, worth it just to hear the snap and the water and the hills, a roller coaster I'm always riding.

How do I know this was not projection, wild fantasy, or even idle speculation? How do you know when the significant person, event, emotion will appear before you like an outstretched hand? How do you know when life opens and then folds in, pointing toward the light, a beam that you will float on, the wave that will carry you to your grave? You know. You know the difference between desperate longing and accepting the fate that is yours.

We both moved slowly because there was all the time in the world.

It was not so much a result of who I was. It was more like who I'd chosen to become. I would never be able to realize all of the possibilities. And I saw this one, my life with this man who ran a café by the ocean. I am much better by water, by salt, by that rhythm; it calms me, soothes me, keeps me cool. Only there could I stay with one person, have a life, the shape of a life like many others, and only in the details would I make it mine.

Finally, when I was ready, I went to the café. I applied for a job. Our eyes met, he took me aside, pressed his palm in mine. He knew, just as I did, the choices we were to make, the possibilities we would have to throw away like dried flowers. He told me to come back Monday. I could start then. Busing tables, taking orders, pouring coffee.

This man at the café. He was not you and he was not not-you. He was someone else, a stranger I could live with in an old house, and one day, a baby, a child. I am not projecting. I am creating. Me with my short hair and big eyes, one day I would have a child, a daughter, who, except for her father's eyes, would look just like me. Her mother. Not you. This does not have to do with you. This is mine. This man in the cotton shirt and sad eyes was mine.

We had a future with a future. A baby who burps and spits and strains our patience, a baby who will grow up to hurt us, remind us of our mistakes, our humanness. This is what I wanted with the man in the restaurant. Our child would not be beautiful and that was a blessing.

In the future, if I saw someone else I was attracted to I would turn my head, shut my eyes, look away, because that is what you must do when you choose marriage and a child because that is what I'm talking about.

But when I came back that Monday, ready to begin a new life, ready for this chosen self, I saw the crowds and the smoke and my stomach fell when I heard the word fire. We grow green and red and then it's ash, fuzzy gray, nothing but death.

Fire is not good, the heat makes me wild, brings out my frantic side, fire brings panic, claustrophobia, death. Fire is too many memories, too much pain, dry skin, parched leaves, snapped twigs, ash disguised as fog.

They said arson. Rags soaked in gasoline. I could not bear to find out if he had started it or someone else had. So then, not too long ago I was in San Francisco, surveying the singular certainty of my future for the first time. By fate, destiny, or mathematical probability, my life had become something by virtue of what it would not be.

But before that, before my separation, my rebellion, before that was the church. Tradition, the small church with its choir balcony, stained glass, and old wood smells. After the service, you would gather the music, slip your feet back into your pumps, shake your hand with the choir members, and then, holding my hand, through the back way of the church, work your way to our old Chevy, parked in the back. You wanted to avoid the minister's hand shake, the chit chat. Your work was done.

Despite your playing at the church, there was no Bible in the house, no prayer before meals, no crosses above our wooden twin beds. There was only music, music played on the record player, the radio, your piano when we pretended I was asleep.

Your music. How could I know that passion? I wanted to be like the other girls, wear makeup, eat cookies. I wanted to be the most important thing to you. But many times when I walked in and found you humming, scribbling notes on white paper, you jumped when I tapped your shoulder, then focused slowly on the girl in front of you, curled and ribboned, trying to discern who I was.

Your mouse-colored hair falling past your ears, covering your eyes, your nubbed pencil, the eraser dust, dark notes pressed into songs, your secret language. What were those songs? Loud deafening, a crescendo, the way you lifted your arms in the air, quickly, violently, then silence.

My piano lessons. Every afternoon after school. You were not a martyr. You were a spiritual person, as evidenced by the modest two-bedroom house we lived in. Only the shiny grand piano, dusted daily, tuned regularly, was money. The piano's sound, so soft then loud I wanted to cry, seemed hedonistic compared to our surroundings. Everything else was secondhand: scraps, noodles, cheese, powdered milk.

I wore the gingham and floral dresses you sewed, dresses pressed and starched every morning. When I was young, the socks turned down, little anklets and patent leather shoes. Later, knee socks and lace-ups, short dresses vulnerable to a flip, a gust of wind that exposed my underwear, my bare thighs. I wanted pants like the other girls wore, girls whose hair was neatly combed or pulled back with a ribbon, girls, who, if I looked closely enough, had purple crusts of jelly around the corners of their mouths.

Most of the days of my life are forgotten. Most of my moments are not even a dream. I will not remember the days I must have been quietly happy. The days I woke up, went to school, and kissed you good night.

In high school I wore jeans like the others and put my makeup on in the girl's bathroom. I'd scrub it off before I came home. By then I knew that you were strange and eccentric with your singular passion for church music. I was embarrassed and mistrustful of you. I told you that I would no longer go to church because I didn't believe in God.

But what about the music, you asked.

It does nothing for me, I said.

I know that's what made you cry sometimes, that I didn't love that music, your music, the sounds of saints, the music of God. But you were beyond me. I couldn't touch you because you had your music. You had the divine.

I am trying to rely on my unreliable memory. Your

hands brushing my hair, scratching my back, running the bath water, carefully turning pages of a book. Still I must ask if even what I remember was real. I remember only what I must. I dream what I don't want to remember. And I must tell you, these days I don't dream of drowning, instead I dream of fire.

When I was four I watched our neighbor's house burn from my bedroom window. My own tiny room so safe, yet close enough to smell the smoke. The neighbors, indistinct in the night, huddled, their mouths collectively forming soft Os. I'm sure I saw you, Mother, in your burgundy choir robe leading them in song. Your arms rose and fell in short staccatos as you pushed yourself up so the music could rise with the heat. Then I heard sounds from the living room piano, the music crescendoing, the tempo increasing. When I looked out the window again, your apparition had vanished with the smoke. The fireman sprayed his hose until the air was ash. The neighbors dispersed, trudging home in their slippers and cotton pajamas while you continued playing in the living room.

And then I was in the future, in this very moment, when they told me you were dead, which meant I could no longer tell you everything, and I was floating, watching myself, a solitary stubborn woman who had not come to terms with the small tragedy that was her life, and her mother, Elizabeth, also solitary but not hard, full of forgiveness before the sinner had even sinned, ready to forgive everyone their sins because she had her music, that part of her not caught in time.

TALISMANS

FÜR ELISE

When she saw Mrs. Dyson in the baggage claim waving a manila envelope as if it were a flag of surrender, Elise wondered if her own capitulation had been a mistake. But why would it be? In San Francisco she was jobless with few friends and fewer prospects, but here in Fairfax, Virginia, she had a house, and, through the casual networking of her high school friends, a job if she wanted. Yet now, as Mrs. Dyson trilled Elise's name, Elise wondered if being homeless and unemployed on the other side of the country might still have its advantages.

Even though Elise's mother's funeral had been a month ago, Mrs. Dyson embraced Elise with the force of someone in full mourning. Mrs. Dyson wore a loose, black dress with scalloped short-sleeves that bound her fleshy, maternal arms. Her auburn hair was curled and sprayed, her face bare except for the swath of red lipstick that matched her nails. As she hugged Elise, Mrs. Dyson pressed the manila envelope stiffly against Elise's back.

"All alone in this world. An orphan," she said, with sharply spearmint breath.

"I always wanted to be an orphan," Elise whispered to no one.

When she was eight, her mother had taken her to a local production of *Little Orphan Annie*. For a month after the show Elise had fantasized about being an orphan; after all, she was already halfway there. Perhaps her mother would die in a car crash, and her own photo would run in the paper along with the headline: "Local Girl Orphaned After Grisly Car Accident." Elise had learned the word "grisly" from the TV news, and she liked the sound of it, sharp, angry, red. A bald, old man, rich and lonely, would see her picture and adopt her. Elise would forget her ghost father who would fade away from memory, leaving not even his shadow. She'd live with her new rich father in a big house from where she'd be driven to school in a limousine with tinted windows. Eventually she would introduce her new father to her third-grade teacher who wore yellow pantsuits that accented her shag haircut. They'd fall in love and marry, and then her new mother would let Elise wear jeans to school like the other girls. Elise would keep by the bed a small photo of her real mother, the one where her hair was loose and long and she held her two-year-old daughter in a matching violet dress tightly on her lap. As her new mother watched, Elise would kneel and pray to God that her old mother had made it to heaven.

The grisly car crash had come fifteen years too late, and now Elise was too old to get a new mother.

Mrs. Dyson released her and placed Elise's hands on the envelope reverently.

"Your mother's legacy. Her immortality. There is much to tell you." Then Mrs. Dyson took the envelope back and slipped it in her tote.

Elise wanted to get home so she could decide what to do with the rest of her life. She had not owned a car in San Francisco, and since her mother's old Ford had been totaled in the accident, she was at the mercy of Mrs. Dyson, who was already briskly walking to the airport's parking garage. She opened the door to the aging Lincoln, the scent of smoke and yeasty booze buried under evergreen air freshener.

"We'll get you home and have a little chat about that envelope. But first a quick stop by the church. They've packed away your mother's stuff in boxes."

Elise rubbed her temples and sank into the passenger's seat. In addition to the two large suitcases that were crammed into the Lincoln's trunk, the rest of her life was in four boxes en route from San Francisco.

Before the funeral Elise had not been in the church since she'd graduated from high school six years ago, but nothing had changed. The church was neither modern nor traditional in its architecture, but rather a hodgepodge of the two. The sanctuary housed long uncomfortable benches and intricate stained-glass windows. The cross with its sleek design and modern staining had a contemporary feel, as did the pulpit. The choir loft held an ancient organ and gray folding chairs whose pads rested on a thinning carpet. For as long as Elise could remember, this had been her mother's world.

Elise withdrew into the sunken seat of the Lincoln. At the funeral there had been a girl in the choir who had sung a heartfelt yet overwrought solo. Even the girl had to stop twice during the song to regain her voice. Her cheeks gleamed from the lights above her and brought everyone to tears. Everyone except Elise. She could feel the congregation's judgment, that she'd been an ungrateful daughter, a cold, callous bitch.

After the funeral, the minister had told Elise that

her mother had gotten the girl, whose name was Carol, off of drugs and given her a new life through the choir.

"Treated her like she was her own daughter," the minister had said as he walked Elise to Mrs. Dyson's car.

Now the church was empty except for an Asian woman waxing the floors in the dim hall light. Like any old office building after hours, Elise thought. They walked up the stairs to the choir loft where the boxes were.

When she was six, Elise had sat up in the choir loft with her mother as she directed the Christmas Eve candlelight service. After the sermon, each congregation member received a white candle stuck through a piece of slotted cardboard. One by one the members touched candles to pass the flame around. Her mother was bent over the organ, her face damp from concentration, so she didn't see Elise when she slipped away downstairs to get her own candle. She scooted into a space in the back pew just as the last candles were being lit. She held her candle steady as an old man dipped his toward hers, until her wick caught his flame. She turned toward the choir loft. Her mother hovered above the organ, bringing music up out of the church, her hands rising and falling in short staccatos. Elise wanted to return before her mother discovered she'd disappeared. Elise slipped into the hall and opened the door to the choir loft. Using her candle for light, she walked up the darkened stairs.

Now the choir loft was lit from the overhead fluorescents Mrs. Dyson had turned on at the base of the stairs. The metal chairs were folded against the wall. The organ was missing, leaving only indentations from the legs, smooth discs flat in the carpet. Two battered cardboard boxes sat where her mother used to direct.

"They're putting in a dreadful pipe organ," Mrs. Dyson said. "In your mother's name, which is the last thing she'd have wanted. Carol's the ring leader. That girl has some nerve. She was on skid row not too long ago and now she acts like she's some gift from God." Mrs. Dyson snorted. "A pipe organ. Of all things."

Elise bent down to examine the boxes. Old choir books were tossed in along with legal pads of her mother's penciled notations. A white coffee mug with the words "Sing to the Lord a New Song" rested on top of the other box, which held a variety of songbooks for Christian musicals for children. After Elise had moved away, first to college, then to San Francisco, her mother had taken on the role of Children's Choir Director in addition to the running the adult choir. Whenever they talked on the phone, it seemed her mother was always involved in a new children's production, usually involving the Old Testament: Noah and the ark, Joseph and the coat of many colors, Moses leading the chosen ones out of Egypt.

"If you can carry the lighter box I'll take the heavier one," Elise said, already straightening up.

Mrs. Dyson toddled over to the box and groaned as she picked it up. "You haven't said anything about the pipe organ."

Elise was halfway down the stairs. "I can't imagine her playing it."

"Amen to that."

They placed the boxes in the back seat since the trunk was full. Elise rolled down her window to get some air.

"One more stop, and then we'll get you home and have our little chat," Mrs. Dyson said as they pulled out of the church driveway.

"Is it necessary?" Elise knew she sounded peevish, but she wanted to get home.

"Oh I think so."

A few miles down the road past the usual array of strip malls and fast food restaurants, Mrs. Dyson turned into the cemetery where Elise's mother was buried.

"I wanted to show you all the flowers people have left her. Lord she was loved." Mrs. Dyson wiped the corner of her eye before she opened her door.

The girl who had sung at her mother's funeral was at the gravesite, kneeled in prayer. Her voluminous dress covered her pregnancy, a fact Elise had not noticed at the funeral.

"She *would* be here," Mrs. Dyson said as they walked up the hill. "Always the scene stealer."

The girl was Elise's age, but seemed more fragile in the late afternoon light. Her lips moved with the fervency of someone intent on salvation. She either didn't hear them approach or ignored them, as she continued her incantation over the grave with clasped hands.

The grave was dotted with small bunches of flowers, most of them dried and shrunken, drained of color. Her mother's favorite flower, the cornflower, was absent. Perhaps, Elise thought, she was the only person still alive who knew that was her mother's favorite. A fresh clump of lilies rested against the tombstone, which had the same epigraph as the mug in the cardboard box in the back seat of Mrs. Dyson's Lincoln. Elise wondered if she should bury the mug there.

Mrs. Dyson cleared her throat. "Well, well, well, look who's here."

The girl looked up and squinted into the sun. "Elise,"

she said softly. She stood up and hugged her. "I'm sorry we didn't talk at the funeral. You disappeared so fast. Of course I understand, it being your mother and all."

Elise stared at the girl. Now that she was closer she recognized the brown eyes, the mousy hair that once must have been honey blonde.

"Carol Mason," she said slowly.

She laughed. "I guess you wouldn't recognize me. That's what you get, moving way out to San Francisco." She held out her hand to show a thin silver band. "I'm married to Chris Hitchens. I'll introduce you to him at church on Sunday."

The last time she had seen Carol was at a party the summer before Elise left for college. Carol had been friendly then in that metallic abstract way people were when they were high.

"Carol is one of the star soloists in our choir," Mrs. Dyson said. "She's so good the rest of us hardly have a chance to sing anymore."

"That's not true." Carol patted Mrs. Dyson's shoulder. "And even if it was, it's got nothing to do with me. My voice is just God's instrument to sing his praises." Carol moved her arm to Elise's shoulder. "Your mother was a special person. Without her I'd probably be dead in the gutter somewhere. I just never was the same after Mark's death."

That was the other funeral they had both attended the summer after eighth grade. Only that time Elise and Carol had gotten high on the hill near the church while her mother played the organ inside.

"Congratulations on your marriage," Elise said. "And the baby." The words sounded empty to her, but she didn't know what else to say.

"Praise to God." Carol absently rubbed her stomach. Her smile was wide and tight, verging on the hysterical.

After they left the cemetery, Mrs. Dyson drove to Elise's house. When she pulled up in the driveway, she turned off the ignition but did not open her door. "We have something to discuss." Elise waited for her to continue, but instead Mrs. Dyson sighed heavily and got out of the car. "But first a drink."

Her hands slid into an outside pocket on her tote bag, which was encircled by a rainbow and the words "Love is a rainbow of beautiful feelings." She pulled out a silver cross that was attached to a chain of keys. Mrs. Dyson opened the door and extended her arm, as if showing Elise the house for the first time. "I took the liberty of straightening it up yesterday. One less thing for you to worry about."

Elise stepped into a place that was a brighter, cleaner version of her childhood. The usual film of dust was absent from the coffee table and bookcase. The hall carpet that led to the two bedrooms and the bathroom was spotless and smelled vaguely of shampoo. The piano looked awkwardly naked without the piles of sheet music and pencils usually scattered about. Her mother had needed to be able to reach anywhere, right, left, up, down for a pencil to scribble her inspirations before they evaporated or hardened like wax. Shiny coasters of Bach's and Beethoven's portraits, new additions to the house since the funeral, rested on the end tables beside the couch and on the piano. It was if her mother had been scrubbed out of existence.

When Elise was in the eighth grade her mother finally admitted that Elise had neither the proclivity nor interest in the piano and let her quit her lessons.

The last song she learned was Beethoven's "Für Elise." Her namesake. Her mother had swayed on the piano bench as Elise played the song from memory, without rhythm, pausing in the wrong moments. Her mother often hummed the song as she spread mayonnaise on their sandwiches or stirred macaroni and cheese in a charred pot on the stove. Even after Elise quit her piano lessons, her mother sometimes played the song in the space of weekend afternoons while Elise hid in her room reading teen magazines with determined indifference, pretending her mother was not playing for her.

Mrs. Dyson took the manila envelope from her tote and placed it on top of the piano. She scurried to the kitchen. "What'll you have?" she called above the clank of ice cubes and running faucet.

"Water's fine." Elise sat on the piano bench and touched the polished wood that covered the keys, and then rubbed her fingers along the edge of the piano bench.

"I've been no stranger to sorrow myself, what with Mr. Dyson's untimely death ten years ago and my barren womb," Mrs. Dyson called from the kitchen. "Still, they say the Lord only gives us what we can bear. Your mother had her share of hard times, but at least she had you." Mrs. Dyson set Elise's glass on the Bach coaster on top of the piano. "And her music, of course."

After easing herself on the couch, Mrs. Dyson took a long gulp from her drink. She wrinkled her brows until they met in a frown. She waved her hands wildly as Elise took a sip of her own drink. Even with the ice there was more gin than water. She wondered if Mrs. Dyson had already been drinking when she'd picked her up at the airport.

"You've got the wrong drink, honey," Mrs. Dyson said.

They exchanged glasses, and Mrs. Dyson reclined again on the couch, closing her eyes. "Ah, nothing like a little drink after a long day," she murmured.

Elise opened the piano lid. Her hands hesitated above the keys. The white notes were like fingers, still and certain, waiting to come to life. She pressed the C key, slowly, so that it wouldn't make a sound.

Mrs. Dyson reached for her glass and tipped it back. "Another?"

"I'm fine. You said you had something to discuss?"

"Soon as I top this off." Mrs. Dyson stood with a groan and carried her glass into the kitchen. Elise was tired, yet she suddenly didn't want to be alone in this house. For when she was alone she would have to decide what to do with the rest of her life.

Her fingers spread to form an unknown chord. She touched the keys. "Für Elise." That familiar beginning heard in elevators, supermarkets, and doctor's waiting rooms everywhere. Two notes repeated, the tension palpable, then the rush of the other notes, uncontrolled and unbidden until before she realized it, she was at another place entirely. Then the two notes returned, bringing her back to where she had started.

She wanted to remember the rest of the song, but it would not come.

Mrs. Dyson returned with her refill and sat on the bench beside Elise. She picked up the manila envelope and waved it as she had done at the airport.

"Her masterpiece." She extracted a sheaf of music and presented Elise with the title page which read "Jesus and the Resurrection."

"She had just finished her own musical," Mrs. Dyson continued. "The kids were going to do it next spring. It was her debut as a children's church music composer."

She thumbed through the music. "A genius, that's what she was." Her hands rested on a page. "Listen to this. This is Mary Magdalene when she finds Jesus at the grave: *Who is it then, who? Who?*" Mrs. Dyson sang in a high watery voice. "And here's Jesus." She lowered her voice an octave. "*Can't you see? I've come from death to show you God's love.*"

Mrs. Dyson pressed her lips together and sniffed. She handed Elise the sheaf of music and then sat back down on the couch, spreading herself expansively.

"I'd like to—with your blessing—direct the musical myself this spring. As a tribute to Elizabeth. The show will go on." Mrs. Dyson rummaged through her tote. She uncapped a silver tube of cherry lipstick and applied the color in two strokes. She fished out a crumpled tissue and blotted her lips. "I'm going to make her a star."

"I don't know," Elise said. She scanned the music, trying to get an idea if the work was any good.

The doorbell rang. Mrs. Dyson jumped up to answer, as if she'd put on her lipstick just for this moment. "Why, look who's here," she said slowly as she opened the door.

Carol waved to Elise from the doorway. "After I saw you at the cemetery, I remembered there was something I wanted to talk to you about."

"Come in," Elise said from the piano bench.

"Just for a minute."

Mrs. Dyson went back to the couch and picked up her drink.

Carol handed Elise a notebook decorated with

rainbows and music notes and hearts. It reminded her of the projects they used to do in elementary school.

"Your mama wrote a musical."

"'Jesus and the Resurrection.'" Elise took the notebook from Carol's thrust-out hands.

"You've heard." Carol glanced at Mrs. Dyson. Her glass held only ice, and her lips had disappeared.

"It's a fake!" Mrs. Dyson stood. She picked up the sheaf of music Elise had left on the piano and waved it in the air. "I've got the original. She gave it to me!"

"We'd started working on the production together before she died," Carol continued. "There's one part for an adult in it. Your mother wanted me to play it."

"Slattern!" Mrs. Dyson lurched toward Carol who was standing next to the piano and grabbed her elbow. She teetered forward and pulled Carol with her onto the floor. The pages of music fell around them, in disarray. Elise picked up Carol's notebook, which she had dropped on her way down.

They lay on the floor for a half minute. Carol was on her back breathing heavily. Mrs. Dyson whimpered on her side.

"My baby! The bitch hurt my baby!" Carol rolled over and slapped Mrs. Dyson, but she didn't stand up.

"You don't deserve none of it," Mrs. Dyson whispered. She was crying beneath the mask of her hands.

Elise gathered the loose pages on the floor. She now had Mrs. Dyson's and Carol's copies of her mother's work. She had not decided if she would give them back.

Elise wondered if God had saved her mother from these people. From her own daughter. She wanted, then, to cover her mother's grave with cornflowers, so that she'd be blanketed in the color of peace. She wanted to sell the house. She wanted to go back to the airport and fly far away, never to return.

Elise's last conversation with her mother had been a month before she died.

"I'm sorry I don't call you more often," Elise had said, as always.

"It's okay. I don't worry about you because of your music." Her mother's voice was faint on the line.

"My music?"

"Those times you played 'Für Elise' on the phone. Not a word from you, just the beginning of the song. Always made my day."

Elise hadn't responded. It was easier to be the daughter her mother had wanted her to be, even if just for that moment. Perhaps the person who played the song on the phone was someone from the children's choir. Or a telemarketer with canned music in the background. Or Mrs. Dyson. Or Carol. Or her imagination. But that person wasn't Elise.

The two women still lay on the floor, limbs splayed in unnatural poses, frozen, as if stunned by a sudden blinding light. Elise returned to the piano. She placed her mother's music on her lap. She closed her eyes. Soft fingers ran through her hair then rested on her cheek.

And then she was playing the first two notes of "Für Elise" over and over, waiting for the rest to come.

FÜR ELISE

PART 2

THAT GIRL

She was captured by his smile, quick, yet sensuous, even before she called his name. The corners of his mouth seemed to kiss his eyes. Elise welcomed something so unrestrained and effortless in her life.

"Young Soo Kim." Elise pronounced each word distinctly. The secretary at the language institute had transcribed the students' Korean names into English letters so that it would be easy for the western teachers to call roll.

"Call me Danny," he said. "That was my nickname in Australia."

"So you've been abroad?"

"Only Australia. G'day, mate." He touched the tip of his gold hoop earring.

The class laughed, and Elise gratefully joined them, relieved she had an ally. To Koreans, a "good atmosphere" could make or break anything: a class, a work group, a family, a relationship.

That night back in her small western-furnished room, Elise slipped her grandfather's pea coat over her naked body, even though the floor was burning hot. She was one of millions in this city of concrete and crowds, all packed in block-style buildings, a city blanketed in a protective gray haze. Behind the city, mountains that she couldn't see sloped gently toward the horizon. Sitting cross-legged on the fake-wooden floor, she shut her eyes and tried to imagine Seoul when it had been the war-torn, poverty-stricken city her grandfather had fought for. But when she erased the cars, shopping bags, suits, coffee shops, and department stores from her imagined landscape, there was nothing left to take its place.

That first week of class she gathered the bits and pieces about Danny, filing them away for some yet undetermined use. Like many of the students at the language institute, he had graduated from college and was studying English to improve his employability. He told the class he was twenty-six in Korean age, twenty-five in western age, and had briefly been in a heavy metal cover band his last year at university. He also alluded to a wounded heart, which gained his classmates' sympathy and admiration, adding to his class mystique. Whenever the students were getting bored, she depended on Danny to bring them back to her with a joke or his smile.

The second week they studied third conditionals. The students went around the circle making sentences. "If I were President of the United States I would…If I were a millionaire I would…" When it was Danny's turn, everyone waited to see what kind of joke he would make.

"If Elise weren't my teacher, I would be her boyfriend." Danny leaned back in his chair, reveling in the shouts and catcalls of his classmates: "You are playboy!" "Danny loves our teacher!"

"He could never be my boyfriend," Elise said, smiling. "The Korean girls would be jealous of me."

The students laughed louder, and Elise called a break ten minutes early so everyone could calm down.

The third week the students wanted an "out class"— which meant they wanted to bond and drink beer under the pretense of using English in the real world. In the other classes she'd taught she'd waited until the last night of the course as was customary, but she liked this class and figured their English was good enough to spend a few hours with them in a more relaxed setting.

The February nights still had a deep chill, and Elise drew her pea coat closer as the class walked past the broken sidewalks, neon signs, and cluttered shop fronts to a bar she had never been to but looked like all the rest. They sat on plastic sofas that surrounded a table expansive enough to hold the fruit, French fries, and dried squid for *anju*, pitchers of OB Lager, and bottles of *soju* they had ordered. Danny was responsible for organizing the drinking games and making sure Elise's glass was full. He sat between Elise and the aspiring flight attendant, whose hand grazed the top of Danny's leg when he spoke to her. For that first hour they played simple drinking games in English. When he lost, Danny would say "shit" or "fuck," then apologize to Elise immediately.

"When I get drunk I swear in English. It's my habit. I feel very free."

"Just be careful. If you say that to an American guy, he might fight you."

Everyone laughed, including Danny. After the games, Danny and the flight attendant girl talked intensely in Korean. Elise turned her back to them and instead engaged with the group of students who were eager to know everything about her. She fed them the details she knew they wanted: that she was from Virginia where they had four seasons just like Korea, that she had lived in San Francisco after college, that the boy she had secretly loved since grade school died in the eighth grade. Her students felt immensely sorry for her then. In Korea, first love was everything.

Elise limited herself to two beers and two shots of *soju*, until finally at one o'clock, she reached for the pea coat nestled between her and Danny and stood to put it on. The students rose as well.

"Where are you going?" Danny asked her as he helped her with her coat.

"It's late. I need to get home," she said.

"It's early," Danny said.

"Your coat looks very warm," the girl beside Danny said.

"It is," she said. "It was my grandfather's. Then my father's." She reached inside the coat pocket and quickly stroked the half photo of her father, glassy-eyed in front of a hut in Thailand.

The students were silent. Months later when they talked about that night, Danny told her what they had all been thinking then: why would a rich American girl wear an old man's coat? She didn't tell him that the coat was from the Korean War, because she feared he would love her or hate her or pity her for the wrong reasons.

The students half-bowed to her before they sat back down and resumed their drinking. Danny and two of his friends from class walked her out to get her a taxi.

As they emerged from the bar, a girl in a short, black skirt with long, straight hair walked out of the night club next door arm-in-arm with a man in a dark, collarless suit.

The girl turned and clapped her hand over her mouth when she saw Danny. Danny stepped toward her, but his friends grabbed him and spoke harshly in Korean to him. Danny broke away and ran toward the guy she was with, their elbows still linked.

"That girl! That girl!" Danny yelled in English.

"His old girlfriend," one of his friends said to Elise.

"Fuck you, bastard!" Danny threw his weight on the guy, toppling them both onto the pavement.

The girl yelled in Korean as she slumped to the ground. Danny's friends grabbed him again, pulling him away. The other guy lay flat, his white shirt half open and spotted under the lamplight. The girl crawled over to the guy and fell on top of him, crying dramatically onto his heaving chest. The streetlight framed them as if they were in a movie. The girl struggled to pull the guy up, and Danny lunged for him again, but his friends came between them, and the girl pulled her new boyfriend away. Danny vomited on the street as Elise approached him.

"Women. Always big problem." He started a smile that ended in a wince. He wiped his mouth.

Elise had to hold her hands in small fists to keep from reaching out and touching his cracked lips, his bleeding knuckles, his rapidly swelling eye. She wanted to touch his pain so that she might feel it herself.

His friends assured her they would take care of everything. They were embarrassed for Danny, and for her, they said. A teacher should not see such things. One of Danny's friends hoisted him on his back, while the other called two taxis, one for Elise, and the other to take Danny home.

She hoped he would explain things to her the next week, but Danny didn't return. That last week the classroom felt cold, and the students waited for her to fill the gap, but she couldn't do it alone.

She saw him a few days after that class had ended. She was at a coffee shop near the institute when she saw him staring at her through the glass. He waved at her and she pointed to the empty chair across from her.

He was smoking a cigarette and wore a leather jacket, making him look already much older than he had in class. He dropped the cigarette on the sidewalk then came in and sat across from her.

"Long time, no see," she said with a tight smile. She could smell the cold air and cigarette smoke on him, a welcome respite from the stuffy coffee shop.

Danny looked down at the floor. "I know. So sorry I didn't come back to class. I was shameful about the fight."

"The class missed you." She sipped her coffee, which tasted like burned water.

"Me too." He kept his hands in his leather jacket pockets, but glanced at her before averting his eyes again.

"Koreans hate taking off their coats. Why?"

Danny shrugged. "I don't know. We are more comfortable keeping them on." He paused. "Why do you wear your father's coat?"

She smoothed the collar of the coat, which was

draped across the cushioned chair she was sitting in. She compulsively checked to make sure the photo of her father was still in the right pocket. "I'll tell you about my coat if you tell me about your fight."

"Okay Teacher."

"I'm not your teacher anymore." Elise signaled the waitress over and ordered two more cups of coffee. "I'll go first."

The coffee arrived in cream-colored china cups adorned with pale delicate roses. Danny poured the straw-shaped sugar and creamer packets into his coffee and stirred with the teaspoon on the saucer.

"I have no family. This coat reminds me of them."

Danny stirred his coffee. "You are a..." He paused and looked upward to find the word, "orphan?"

Elise smiled. "Orphan is a word for children. But yes, you could say so."

"Oh my God. So terrible."

"It's okay." She wanted to reach out and pat his hand. "My father died when I was a baby. He wore this coat to remember his father. I wear it to remember him."

"What about your mother?"

Her throat tightened. "She died recently. I don't need anything to remember her."

She fingered the ashtray Danny had been eyeing. "You can smoke. It's okay."

"Thanks." He removed a pack of 88 Lights from inside his jacket and lit his cigarette, turning his head away from her each time he exhaled.

"So tell me about that fight," she said.

Some classmates from the institute called his name in Korean from a nearby table. Danny stood and bowed slightly to them, said a few words, then sat back down. He leaned forward as if to whisper.

"Not here. Too many people."

"Where, then?"

"How about a video room? Have you ever been?"

"No." She stirred her black coffee with the small tea spoon.

"We can talk there."

"All right then," she said. "If that's what you want."

He smiled, confident again. "Yes. Very much."

She met him after work that night. The room, she later learned, was like thousands of video rooms in Korea. The wallpaper, in floral pastels, buckled where the concrete wall was cracking underneath. They sat across from the TV on a couch made of hard, pale plastic that matched the wallpaper. As the opening credits of *The Terminator* began rolling, a movie they'd both seen before, Danny poured the Cass beer he had brought in. He opened the bags of snacks he'd bought to eat with the beer. They toasted, and the Cass, warm and tasteless, disappeared from their tiny paper cups. Elise picked up a chip from the open bag on the table and put it directly on her tongue.

"Oh, it's sweet."

Danny crunched on a chip and smacked his lips dramatically. "Delicious."

She took a fried ring from the other bag and held it up. "And what's this?"

"Squid flavor. Very good."

She popped it in her mouth. "Not too bad." She reached for another ring.

"You are getting adjusted to Korea."

As soon as she drained another cup of beer, Danny finished his and refilled their cups.

"So tell me about that fight. You called your old girlfriend 'that girl' in English. Why?"

"In Korean we say *ke yuja*. That's what we call a girl we don't know well. She's not our girlfriend yet. Using real name is too close. I wanted to show I didn't care about her." He closed his hands. "That's the funny thing. I don't care about her. But I had to fight the guy."

"Why?"

"Korean way I guess." He shrugged. "Mind if I smoke?" he said as he pulled a pack out of his jacket, which made noises each time he shifted. She shook her head. "My parents, they want me to find a job and then marry. But I don't want that right now."

Elise sat back and folded her legs on the sofa. "What do you want then?" she asked.

"I want to be free." He tapped his cigarette on the black plastic ashtray next to his beer and set it down.

"You're lucky you have parents who love you."

"Sometimes it is a kind of burden." Danny met her eyes briefly, then laughed. "But it's my duty. What can I do?"

She noticed then that a shock of hair had escaped from the gelled spikes artfully arranged along his scalp. Instinctively, she smoothed it back down. Her hand lingered. Danny turned to her and rubbed the scabbed part of his knuckles across her cheek. She touched his bruises, the swollen eye, his cracked lips as she had wanted to do weeks before. She wanted to know what it felt like, to fight for no other reason except that not fighting was worse.

"With you I can be free," he said.

She saw him then, this trapped man with a desperate hopefulness that would require more than she could give.

"It's not real, this freedom," she said, standing up. She put her pea coat on, and left the room willing herself to not look back.

If her life were a Korean drama from that year, 1996, Elise would be The American Girl. Koreans associated her blond hair and blue eyes with a light, free-spirit that Koreans, burdened with a long and heavy history, felt they were fated to never have. In the drama, Elise was a stock, minor character whose purpose was to provide comic relief. There would be a funny scene or two of Elise with the students, one with her explaining the pronunciation of "chicken" and "kitchen" on the whiteboard, another with her mistakenly using the low form of language usually reserved for children and dogs to address Korean elders.

In her American show, however, she was counting the minutes until class was over so she could drink with the other teachers in the *hof* across the street, then collapse in bed for a few hours of sleep before the next morning's 6:30 class. Sleep-deprived by the early morning and late evening split shifts, Elise relied on the textbook or easy games the students loved like Password or Jeopardy to make it through that last hour. Yet they liked her, she could tell, because she laughed at their simple jokes and played the part of the American they wanted her to be.

TALISMANS

By mid-April the cherry blossoms were in full bloom, so that the trees looked as if they were covered in snow. She ran into him one night after drinking with her friends in the *hof* across from the institute. She was drunk and wanted to go home. She was still wearing the pea coat even though it was really too warm for it. As she stepped onto the street to hail a taxi she felt a tap on her shoulder. She turned and saw his smile and the hoop earring.

"Danny! What are you doing here?"

"You shouldn't go home alone. It's a little dangerous."

He stopped a cab and got in beside her. He asked her where she lived, and then he gave the driver directions in Korean. He leaned his head against the car's glass and kept his eyes closed for the five-minute ride. When the cab stopped in front of her house, Elise reached for her money, but Danny shook his head and paid for the fare. He walked her to her apartment building.

"Thanks, Danny. You're a gentleman." As she was about to walk in her building, he pulled her close and harshly kissed her. He smelled complicated: a heady mixture of strong cologne, his mother's *kimchi,* cracked leather, and cigarettes.

"Okay?" he asked.

"Okay," she whispered. Her desire collapsed into tight bright circles that chained her to him. She kissed him harder and pressed her body against his.

"With you I can be free," he said again between kisses.

"Describe it, this freedom," she whispered, breathless.

"It smells like your perfume, so small and sweet." He kissed her neck and collarbone. "Like flowers hiding under the wool of your coat."

She held her breath and pulled away. So she smelled complicated, too. She felt that she was under water, and that if she could just make it back to her room she could breathe again.

From her bedroom window she watched him propel himself down the street, fists punching the air as he disappeared into the chill of the night sky.

Elise saw that their story hinted of more than what was allowed on prime-time dramas, that what was to happen would be more than a chaste, discreet love. And, when she thought about it, what else could their story be? The exotic, loose foreigner. The innocent Korean man. Her blond hair, blue eyes, and pale skin. His coarse hair, coffee eyes, skin the color of soybeans. Her moon-shaped breasts, too large for any Korean bras, his hairless body, elegantly lean and muscled. The inevitability of their love, if she could be so bold as to call it that, would bleed into late-night adult drama of illicit sex in seedy hotel rooms and empty side streets.

The next day he paged her. On her break she waited in line at the phone booth outside the institute with the other students. When it was her turn she made sure the phone booth door was closed and dialed his number. A woman's voice answered. Elise asked for Danny in English.

"Elise teacher." His voice sounded like he was an ocean away.

"I'm not your teacher, remember?"

"Yes." There was a long pause. Danny muttered something in Korean and she heard his mother's voice. Elise guessed he was asking his mother to leave the room.

"Danny? I only have a few minutes before my class." She looked at the students in line waiting for the phone, their images smudged by the fingerprinted glass.

"I want to take you somewhere. Just us. Will you come?"

"Danny." She tried to sound surprised. She said what she had rehearsed on the way to school that morning. "I *do* like you. But I can't. It's a mistake. We both know that."

"Sorry." Then the line went dead. Elise blinked and lingered in the booth, listened to the beep of the disconnection. Even dial tones were different here, she thought, as she carefully placed the phone back in its cradle.

He paged her the next day, and the next, but she ignored him. She thought of him all week, of that kiss in the street below her apartment, of the strength of his arms, of how disappointed she was when he wasn't outside the institute or her apartment waiting for her. She knew that if she saw him she would give into his kisses and whatever else he wanted, if he would only try again.

Friday he was waiting for her when she emerged from the *hof* across from her school. She was drunk already and grabbed his arm, determined not to let go.

With the streetlights high and bright, their arms sloppy on each other, they wove between the lovers and friends walking in twos, threes, and fours, until he found the place, a Korean-style love hotel, a *yogwan*, with heated floors and blankets for a bed called a *yo*.

She peeled off her coat and clothes, then put the coat back on. Her hair was loose, just touching the collar of the coat. She pushed him onto the *yo*, and was frantic on top of him. He held her shoulders, trying to slow down.

"Why hurry? We have time," he murmured. She stopped moving then and took off the coat. She lay down beside him and wrapped her arms around him.

"That would be nice," she said. "To believe in time." Their home became an endless string of love hotels, the rooms different yet comfortably the same. Once inside, the door safely locked, they fell on the *yo* together, naked and sweaty, temporarily severed from their lives that continued outside the room.

Once, a few months into their relationship, they were lying together on the *yo* under the blanket watching a typical Korean drama. On the TV, a man was yelling at a girl with a short skirt and long hair who was running away from him in the rain. As she looked back at him, a car drove toward her and knocked her onto the wet pavement. The man held the dying girl, cursing heaven in the rain with a raised fist.

"Why do people like these shows?"

"That is maybe because of Korean *han*."

"*Han?*"

"I can't translate into English. It is a part of Korea because of our sad history."

"What does it mean?"

Danny drank his beer and licked his lips. Elise suspected he was going to say something that may not be true, just to quiet her. "*Han* is longing and sadness for something or someone that you can't have. In the past, many lovers were parted forever. Now, the older generation feels *han* because Korea is divided. My generation, we have no memories of family in North Korea. So we don't feel *han*."

"So why do you watch these shows? Can't people just be happy and in love?"

He felt for the pack of 88 Lights next to the glass he had set down and lit a cigarette. "We remember sad endings much longer than happy ones."

"Was that how it was with your ex-girlfriend?"

"I guess so," he said. "That was more like *jung*. Hard to translate. Affection. But more like bond. How you say, like bondage? With her, with my family. It means that you can't let go."

She took the cigarette from him and inhaled, savoring the wet filter where his mouth had been. "How did this all happen?" she asked.

"What?"

She wanted to gesture around the room at the fluorescent lights, the pink wallpaper on the ceiling, the thick blankets in pale green and blue on the warm plastic *ondol* floor. "The break up."

"Same story."

"Not the details."

Now on TV, salarymen were drinking at a hostess bar. Women in heavy makeup and tight shirts poured beer from plastic pitchers as the men drunkenly sang Korean songs of love and longing. Outside the bar, two men waited in a car with tinted windows, their black suits and sunglasses indicating that they were part of the Korean mafia. Whether they were waiting for one of the women or men was unclear to Elise.

Danny drained his glass of beer and glanced at the dorm-sized refrigerator the TV was resting on. Elise obliged, and took out one of the bottles of *soju* they had brought. She poured some into two shot glasses. Danny drank his shot and she refilled his glass. She sipped hers and chased it with beer.

"Okay," he said. He'd met his old girlfriend in college, he told her. She was pretty of course, but what he'd liked about her was her loyalty. She'd written him letters during the two years he was away for his mandatory military service, promising to wait for him. They had planned on getting married when she was twenty-five and he was twenty-seven. After a year of marriage they would start their family and live with his parents, as was the duty of eldest sons. Then, one day she paged him saying she needed to talk, it was urgent. He thought she might be pregnant. Instead, in a coffee shop she broke up with him. She gave no reason, but later he found out she was back together with her old high school boyfriend, her first love.

"Was she your first love?"

"At the time I thought so."

Feeling loose and liquid, Elise slowly crawled on all fours to get the next bottle of *soju*. She knew he was watching her. After she poured two shots, she kissed him full on the mouth.

"Tell me more," she whispered. He placed his hand on her back, then pulled the blanket over them.

At first after the breakup, Danny said, he had paged his old girlfriend five or six times each day. She would sometimes call him back, but only after every third or fourth page. He begged her to give him another chance. He promised to be kinder, more giving, more attentive, more considerate, more loving. He told her he would give her time. That he would wait. He told her he could not live without her. That if she did not take him back he didn't know what he would do. He told her he wanted to die.

Danny held his empty glass up. "More?"

"Please," she said as she filled his glass.

For weeks, Danny spent most nights drunk and despondent in dark clubs that piped Korean techno music and were fringed with made-up girls waiting for someone to buy them drinks. His friends consoled him with shots from expensive bottles of Chivas Regal. They'd never liked his girlfriend much anyway. She was beautiful, yes, but she had always struck them as a bit cold, they confided. Beautiful girls were everywhere. He was better off without her.

So he kept going out with his friends at night, drinking and looking at women. They went to the booking clubs where for 220,000 *won*—about two hundred and fifty dollars—they got a booth, a bottle of whisky and *anju* of fruit, nuts, and dried squid. The fee also included a steady stream of pretty girls that the waiter would bring over to sit at their table for drinks and conversation.

"I should hope so for that money," Elise said. "What else did you do?"

"Sometimes I went on a 'meeting'—like a group date—with my friends." Four of his friends and four girls would sit across from each other and play drinking games. At the end of the evening they would vote in ranking order who was the best potential date. Danny was always first or second. He enjoyed the attention, he admitted, but he just couldn't seem to find a girl he was interested in. They all reminded him too much of his ex-girlfriend.

"But you're over her now?"

"Of course." Danny straddled Elise, placing his elbows above her shoulders. "You are much better."

His kissed her, then rolled onto his back. Elise was not satisfied.

"So how did you know you were over her?"

One morning, he said, he awoke hungry for the first time since his girlfriend had broken up with him six weeks before. He told his mother, and she made him a full breakfast with fried fish and bean paste soup and half a dozen side dishes. He felt as if he was eating his first meal after a long illness. His mother refilled his rice bowl three times.

He told his mother he wanted to take an English class to help him on the civil service exam he was supposed to be studying for, and she gave him an envelope thick with bills to pay for the course. In reality, he was taking his friends' advice. Language institutes were a great way to meet girls.

"So that's when you came to my class."

"That's right. I thought you were very beautiful. Your hair, so curly." He ran his fingers through her hair, slightly matted from sex. "Natural. Not like Korean women."

Elise smoothed his hair, which always had a few

strands out of place, even though he gelled them. She traced the gold hoop in his ear. Soon he would have to start looking for a job, which meant he would have to cut his hair and give up his earring. His face was round and his features too large to look good with a crew cut. Already she mourned the loss.

On TV, the two mafia guys were beating up one of the salarymen in the street.

"Why are they kicking him?"

"He owes them money. And he is fucking the boss's girlfriend." He used words like "fuck" and "bullshit" and "asshole" freely with her now.

"Was that how it was with your girlfriend?"

"No. Not so exciting."

The drama on TV was halfway over. Forbidden lovers were meeting secretly, companies were going bankrupt, and patriarchs were dying of cancer.

"So what about me?" She poured herself another shot of *soju* to loosen the tight spot in her throat.

Danny smiled slightly. It was not the open smile of that first day of class, but a sly, knowing smile.

"You are my first love. Really."

Elise turned off the TV even though the show was not over. She slid into the crook between his chest and arm. He had almost no hair on his body, just a light patch under his arms and no body odor, except for the garlic that sweated from his pores.

Later that night, they sat by the open window, wrapped themselves together in a blanket and shared a cigarette.

Elise pointed to the moon.

"What's that in Korean?"

"*Dahl.*"

"*Dahl,*" she repeated.

She pointed to one of the few visible stars.

"*Byul.*"

"How do you say sky?" she asked.

"*Hana.*"

"*Dahl. Byul. Hana,*" she incanted.

"Do you know what *sarang hayo* means?" He touched her open palm.

She took her hand away and pulled the blanket closer so that her head was hidden from the night sky. "I love you," she whispered into the dark shelter she had made for them.

In late September, Danny invited Elise to his house for the harvest holiday called *Chusok.*

"Why? Your parents don't know about us," she said. They were standing in front of the door to her apartment.

"No. Parents only meet a girl before marriage."

"What if I tell them?" She fished her keys out of her purse.

"What?"

"That I'm your girlfriend. Lover." She turned from him and unlocked the door.

"No," he said loudly. "That is not the way."

"What is the way?" She faced him and wrapped her arms around him.

"Slowly. Step by step. Right now, we are secret." He breathed fast into her ear and neck.

"Well, you know what they say, 'Whoever cannot keep a secret cannot love.'" She pulled away. "What should I wear?"

"Teacher clothes. Of course."

He picked her up in his parents' car. She joked that he looked like a salaryman in his suit and without his earring. She wore a black skirt that grazed the end of her calves and a pale, blue cotton blouse. He asked her to button her blouse up one more so that only her collarbone was exposed, and she did so without arguing.

It was a small gathering, just Danny, his parents, and his paternal grandmother since his younger brother was away for his military service. His parents could speak some English, but his grandmother, wearing the traditional Korean *hanbok*, her gray hair knotted in a bun with a silver stickpin, only stared at Elise throughout the evening. Once she reached up and patted Elise's hair, then quickly withdrew her hand as if she had touched fire.

Before the meal the family paid respects to their dead elders. A small altar with fruit, meat, and traditional rice cakes was set up in the parents' bedroom. There was a black and white photo of a gray-haired man, unsmiling. Danny's father kneeled on the floor and bowed several times. Danny followed. Afterward, Elise asked him in a whisper why his grandmother was crying.

"She still misses my grandfather," Danny said. "She always cries like that when she remembers him."

"My mother never cried like that."

"Maybe she cried alone, so that you would not worry about her."

Elise had thought of that as well, but how could she know her mother's pain if she kept it secret?

They sat on cushions around the low table that was crammed with side dishes of mountain roots and vegetables, *kimchi*, and different kinds of meat. His father told Elise that she used metal chopsticks as well as a Korean. She told his parents she appreciated the home-cooked food.

"I feel sorry for my son's wife," Danny's father said. "They say a son loves his mother's *kimchi* the best." He looked at his wife for approval.

"I'll teach her how to make it," Danny's mother said. Her jeweled hands flashed as she picked up a morsel of meat with her chopsticks. She placed the meat in her mouth without touching her lips, so that her beige lipstick remained intact.

"We worry," his father said. "He needs a girlfriend. Time for him to get a job and get married." Elise wondered if Danny would look like his father one day, scrubbed and shiny with self-importance.

Danny stared into his plate.

"I'm sure he'll meet someone," she said.

"The younger generation is very westernized." He drained his *soju,* and his wife poured another shot as soon as he set the glass down. "They all want a love marriage. But arranged marriage is better. Parents know their children very well. They can know a good match for their child."

Danny drank his *soju* in one gulp. Elise hurried to fill his glass.

"You know Korean custom very well," Danny's father said. He reached over and poured *soju* into Elise's glass.

"Not really," said Elise. She clicked glasses with his

father and they both drank. "But I'm learning."

Afterward, Danny's mother wrapped some rice cakes for Elise to take home. Elise thanked them for dinner.

"*Kamshamnida,*" Elise said to Danny's grandmother. The old woman, red-eyed, nodded in acknowledgment.

Danny was silent as he drove her home.

"Let's go somewhere," she said.

"I can't. My parents, they will worry."

"Can't you call them? Tell them you're going out with your friends. Tell them you're with me."

He shook his head, not looking at her.

"Come upstairs then."

"I told you I can't. Will you fucking listen?"

When he stopped near her apartment, Elise leaned over and kissed him on the cheek. Danny nodded, staring straight ahead, his hands gripping the steering wheel. She closed the door then walked in front of the car toward her building. She listened for the slam of his car door, for he always walked her to her place. By the time she reached the building door she knew he would not come.

She unlocked her door and greeted her roommate and the others from her work. They were drinking, playing cards, listening to music that she'd almost forgotten. She sat with them, took the proffered glass of beer, and began to endure the moments until they would again meet.

Danny reached for the bag of shrimp-flavored chips beside the *yo* they just had sex on. He ripped a corner open with his teeth and waved the bag in front of Elise. She thrust her hand out like she was stopping traffic, and stuck her tongue out.

"Delicious." He popped a handful into his mouth. They smiled at their now familiar joke. He shook a few of the chips into his hand then turned on the TV with the remote. Elise snuggled under the thick blanket beside him.

Danny cracked the window open. He reached for the ashtray on top of the TV and balanced it on the ledge. Even now she was surprised by his body, the compact leanness of it, the guileless way the muscles flexed and relaxed when he moved. She, on the other hand, was thinking about Korean women, how thin and flat they were, and so she tried to lie, sit, and walk in ways that showed her in the most flattering light.

She avoided lying on her side because her breasts and stomach looked like deflated ski slopes. When she was on top of him or on all fours or wearing a low cut top that was loose in the waist—then she looked pretty good.

"I didn't plan on falling in love with you, you know," she said.

"Do you regret?" he asked, trying to sound playful.

"Sometimes. Don't you?"

"No." His voice hardened, and he held her so tight she couldn't breathe. "I will never regret. Because I will never experience this again."

Then she saw it. He would not want the mother of his children to do the things she did.

The next week turned suddenly cold. One day between classes, Elise sat in the coffee shop near the institute. She was wearing her coat, drinking her watery cup of coffee in the delicate china cup, when she looked up and saw them. The sun shone on him and the girl and illuminated them like angels. The girl wore a pink coat with a fur collar and a matching headband. *Innocent,* Elise thought. *Virginal.* They walked past the window, holding hands. Elise stood up to stop him, forgetting for a moment glass lay between them and that he hadn't seen or was pretending not to see her.

Elise sat near the window of the love hotel and tapped out a cigarette. She opened the window to watch for him and blew smoke through the torn screen. She felt that half her life was spent in these rooms waiting for him. He was the one with obligations to friends and family that he must tear away from. Elise's only obligation was her job. She waited patiently; he always came. This time though, she considered that he wouldn't, that he would disappear just as he did after the fight with his ex-girlfriend nine months ago.

Wisps swirled toward where she hoped he might be, then dissipated into the night. She sent the smoke as a signal floating past the string of love hotels identical to the one she was sitting in, through the Seoul streets, over the old women hunched with bundles on their backs, curving through the men in their dark, plain suits and short hair, snaking between the young girls in matching school uniforms, their arms linked in solidarity, until her SOS found him and whispered that she was waiting.

That had been her mother. Waiting for her father's return. Reduced to that. After her mother's death more than a year ago, Elise had reduced her own life to a few boxes now in storage. The items in the boxes had no practical use, but they were things she wasn't ready to let go of: her mother's tarnished silver and chipped china, dusty piano books from the lessons Elise had hated, a photo of her father as a young man caught in a snow storm wearing the pea coat, her father's uniform from Vietnam, her eighth grade yearbook (it had the last picture of the dead boy she'd loved), the shoes her mother was wearing when she died (black leather flats, the heel scuffed and needing to be redone), a photo of Elise as a baby with her father (the only one of them together), a small album of her with her mother over the years, together and separate.

She had discovered the album soon after her mother's death in the top nightstand drawer. The cover was plain, brown leather. The photos, protected by plastic sleeves, were arranged chronologically with the location and date inked on the back. The final page read "The End" in her mother's steady cursive. The last picture was of Elise the day she left for college. She stood between the stuffed duffel bags, hands on hips, hair wavy and long, T-shirt and jeans defiantly tight, a forced smile toward the camera, as if to say: I'm already gone.

He arrived just then, with beer and *soju* and sweet chips, and he took her in his arms and whispered that he loved her, just like the times before. Elise poured beer from a large bottle into the tiny juice-sized glasses, courtesy of the love hotel. She drained hers and poured another, gaining courage.

"Who is she?"

"Who?"

"That girl. The one your parents want you to marry."

"No one." He stared out the window as if he'd suddenly found something important out there.

"Bullshit. I saw you with her. You were walking down the street holding hands like boyfriend and girlfriend."

He walked to her and pushed her on the floor. He fell on top of her, his body wild and frantic. They had fast, hard sex, a kind they had never had before because now he knew what she knew: they were out of time. She licked his skin, pulled his hair, scratched his back— hoping that there would be some part of him, a hair, his sweat, a flake of skin that she could keep. Afterward, he cried like a child, his head on her breasts. She kept her hands fisted, but finally they relaxed, and she stroked his hair.

"Why are you giving up your life for them?"

"It is my duty." He sat up. His eyes were red, his face pale. He smelled like drink and cigarettes. "What do you know about that?"

"More than you fucking realize." She was angry now. She was just getting started. "What about this Korean wife of yours? Huh? Will she put your dick in her mouth and touch your asshole until you come? Huh? How will you get your wife to do that? Huh?" She poked his chest with every "huh," the way she'd seen Koreans do when they were angry.

"Sex is not everything." His voice was flat. He got

up and pushed the window farther open. The cold air reminded her she was naked.

"Such a waste," Elise said. She shook her head. Her throat was tight, but her eyes were clear and dry.

Danny grabbed the pea coat that was on the floor and draped it over himself like a cloak. He lay on his stomach, his face buried in the *yo*, his torso hidden, as if he could will himself to disappear. Perhaps he was waiting for her to come to him, as she always had before.

Instead she moved to the window and smoked until she heard his punctuated snoring. A Korean dial tone, she thought, that's what he sounded like. She dressed quickly then leaned over him. Slowly she extracted from the coat the half photo of her father, and placed it in her jeans pocket. She stood a moment, soaking him in—his criss-crossed hair, smooth shoulders and arms wrapped in her pea coat, his bare legs spread in a V, his face hidden. Then she turned off the light and closed the door, quietly, so as not to disturb him.

TALISMANS

Not far outside Saigon, the minibus veered around another curve, spitting rocks and gravel into the small shrubs and red rock beneath us. I pressed my fingers to the window and imagined our bus skidding off the road and tumbling to the valley below. With each turn of the bus, the world outside would be like a vacation slideshow gone awry: a flash of mint-green rice paddies, then sharp stones, then broken glass, then the oval pond, deep and sparkling like an upside down sky. I would be the only survivor.

"Jesus," the guy sitting beside Jenna said. He hugged his backpack, which had a large Canadian flag sewn on it. "I do not want to die here."

I tucked my thumb into my shorts pocket and rubbed the half-photograph of my father. Jenna adjusted the knot on her red bandana, and touched the silver hoop in her nostril. Tanned and tattooed from the full moon party a few weeks ago on Thailand's Ko Phangan, she was full of enthusiasm for her life-changing experience, and like the recently converted was anxious to share it with anyone and everyone.

"Could you please slow down," the Canadian

pleaded in slow, measured words to our guide, Hai, who twisted to face us.

I rolled my eyes so that Hai would see that I wasn't one of them. The type who paid twenty bucks, meals not included, to travel with their own kind in a beat-up minivan. Westerners who believed they owned the world.

Hai, a slight man with steely, narrow eyes that squinted when he fake-smiled, untwisted and spoke in Vietnamese to the driver, whose neck was creased with rings of dirt like a cut-down tree. The driver nodded, and stepped on the gas. Chastened, the Canadian renewed his interest in Jenna's story. I decided to ignore them the same way in high school I'd ignored the popular kids who thought the world was created for them. At twenty-five, I'd already had lots of practice.

In the seat beside me was a Japanese man with close-cut hair and a smooth, boyish face. He wore a compass looped around his neck that he checked periodically during the ride. He held out his hand for me to shake.

'My name is Kitano," he said in halting English. Even though his grip was weak, he shook my hand enthusiastically. He said he was a salaryman at a big Japanese company and was using his one-week vacation here in Vietnam as his last big adventure before he married one of the secretaries at the company in the fall. Kitano stretched his legs out and fingered the zipper above his knee. His nylon pants were the kind that zipped off into shorts, and the side pockets puckered and bulged with unseen items. "How long you travel?" Like many Japanese, he pronounced his Ls like Rs.

"Until the money runs out. A year if I'm lucky."

"Alone?"

I nodded.

"Why you travel so long time?"

I took the photo out from my shorts pocket and placed it in Kitano's open palm. "This is my father. He was in the war here."

Kitano held the photo close to his eyes and squinted. "He looks like hippie."

"He was then, I guess," I said. "But he was a hero, too." The word "hero" rolled off my tongue like it was true.

Kitano scrutinized the photo, then handed it back to me with a slight nod. He made a scissor motion with his hand. "Why cut in half?"

I ran my fingers along the edge. "That's a secret."

I hadn't figured out how to tell that part of the story yet. The missing half of the photo, I assumed, was of my father's Thai wife. I wasn't sure if she cut herself out before she sent the letter and photo informing my mother of his death, or if my mother, out of spite or sorrow, had taken the scissors from her sewing table and cleanly excised the image, snipping away the other woman like a stray thread on a shirt.

"Have you ever seen *Apocalypse Now*?" I asked.

Kitano shook his head. "No, sorry."

"Well, my father looked like Martin Sheen in the movie—the main character."

"Martin Sheen?"

"A famous actor. Never mind." I was getting nowhere with him. I scanned the bus for someone I could tell my story to who would be appropriately impressed. The seats were packed with large-boned westerners, hung-over and red-eyed, wearing midriffs, T-shirts, and cotton shorts, their bare legs pressed into the tiny seats. An early morning odor of sour milk—white-people sweat—hung in the air. More than anything, they probably wished they were back at their guesthouses, sleeping through their hangovers until late in the afternoon when they would start partying all over again.

Within a few months of travelling in Thailand, Laos, and Vietnam, the scene had become familiar. Most of the backpackers I'd met were in their twenties on a post-college, pre-real-job fling, ready for experience and the tales they came with them. With their slack necks and half-closed lids, the ones on this bus listened to Jenna with half-interest. They had heard her full moon story before, if not her exact story, then another one like it. Even more likely, they had lived the experience themselves and, for the moment, were bored from the telling and hearing of it. So an afternoon of tunnels with the promise of a river sunset would at least bring a new round of stories and shared experiences to the bar that evening, and that was why they had dragged themselves out of bed to endure the heat and western body odor and tight places.

I told myself I could befriend them if I wanted. It wasn't high school anymore, when the Jennas of the world acknowledged me with benign smiles of superiority. I knew the rules now. I could tell them about the restaurant in Saigon that served snake's blood out of shot glasses. That would get them going. That was easy—being half-friends with them for a day. But the longer I traveled, the less I felt like them. *They* couldn't understand that I was on this bus not for some entertaining story I would tell in front of boozy-eyed, sudden friends. What did they know about loss and suffering?

Hai turned to check on us. I saw for the first time that a scar, pale and smooth, sliced his cheek from ear to jaw. I scooted past Kitano and placed my shoulders between the driver and Hai.

"Are we doing okay with the time?"

"On schedule." Something was wrong with the left corner of his lip, which didn't move when he talked, as if a nerve had been cut.

"So we'll make it to the Mekong before sunset?"

"Always do," he said.

"Your English is really good."

"I worked with the Americans in the war."

"Do you like being a guide?"

"It's okay." Hai sighed. He was tired of me. "A government tour guide makes more money. But I can't get one of those jobs. Fought on the wrong side."

No doubt it was true. But the guides had learned what truths to tell and which ones to keep silent about to get the best tips from tourists.

"Where did you fight?"

"All over." Hai smiled slowly like it was painful. The left part of his lip didn't move, so his smile looked cocky, almost sneering. "Now the government builds nice hotels so that you Americans will come and spend your money. We are all friends now. That's what we say."

"Were you on a boat?"

"Boat?" Hai shook his head.

"My father was on a patrol boat here."

"Really?" His voice went up and he half-smiled again.

I looked around to make sure the others weren't listening, but I didn't need to worry. Jenna was holding center stage. I leaned into Hai.

"One night while they were sleeping, their throats were slit. Vietcong, of course." I tried to sound casual, like I wasn't trying to impress him.

Hai cleared his throat. "I'm sorry about your father. It was a long time ago."

"That's why I'm on this trip. To see the Mekong Delta. Where it happened."

"I'm not sure if you'll see much more than what you can in a postcard. But good luck." He faced the front of the van. I returned to my seat like a sullen school child who had just been dismissed by the teacher.

"That's what I'm learning about all this," Jenna said in her seductive British accent. "To just let go. To experience life. Not go so fast." She touched the cloth of her bandana. She was the type who could take a scrap of material and wrap it in such a way that it looked funky and chic at the same time. Jenna was one of those girls I'd watched from afar, the type who was innocent enough to believe that one night of the right combination of people and drugs could bring epiphanies that would last longer than a full moon.

I tried to ignore the chattering and returned to the scene outside my window, where a group of schoolgirls in the traditional *ao dai* were bicycling home from school. That was how I wanted my Vietnam to be: schoolgirls with white, silk tunics and straight bangs, the sun reflecting off the metal of their one-speed bikes, the green-saturated rice paddies shimmering behind them. But if I remembered that only, it would be a lie. For every bicycle there were three scooters, and for every schoolgirl's dress there were ten Coca-Cola T-shirts, and for every rice paddy there were twenty apartment buildings. I decided to try again with Kitano.

"See those stalls out there?"

"Very cheap," Kitano said, reaching for his backpack under his seat. "I buy many things from them."

"My father was in a boat here, just as small as those." I pointed at the passing landscape through the thumb-stained glass. "If you'd seen *Apocalypse Now*," I couldn't help adding, "you'd know the kind of boat I'm talking about."

I could never get enough of Martin Sheen in that opening sequence, waking up in the city he was trapped in, his voice tight as a wire: *still in Saigon*. I wondered if my father had felt that way when he was here: *still on the boat*. Or after that back in the States, before he had gone native: *still at home*. "Still on the bus," I said.

"Still on the bus," Kitano repeated absently. "Look at what I buy."

He took out a Zippo lighter from his front pocket, which he then examined from all angles. He pointed to the message on it. "How do you say this?"

"Death is my business, and business has been good."

He repeated the slogan, trying to imitate my intonation and accent. Then he showed me the postcards he had bought, fanning them like a deck of cards. On the back of each one, printed on the heavy cardboard, were the words "Beautiful Scenes of Vietnam," with the location of each picture written in Vietnamese, English, French, and Japanese. One card depicted a succession of lime-green and ochre rice paddies in front of dark rocks which jutted out like misshapen hills. Behind the hills, brown and faded mountains extended to the edges of the postcard. The water in the rice paddies mirrored the soft sky, and the shrub trees in the foreground with the mountains were reverse-imaged as pale apparitions on green glass. Conspicuously marked by the absence of people, the scene's stillness was more eerie than calm.

The next card showed an emerald lake which spread into a V. Full, round hills a shade deeper than the water bordered the lake. The hills met at the tip of the V in the middle of the card, then were lost in clouds. Floating out of the hills' shadow on the lake toward the viewer were two, small boats narrower than canoes. The Vietnamese sat with umbrellas to shade themselves from the sun, while a man stood at the back of each boat paddling to some destination past the postcard. The third postcard I took from Kitano.

"You want?"

"Can I?" I fingered the border.

"Sure. I don't need." He tapped the disposable camera on his lap. "Here is real photo of schoolgirls on bicycles. You can keep." I put the postcard in my pocket where the photo of my father was. Kitano placed the remaining postcards in his backpack. He leaned across me and clicked a few pictures of the dirt road and shrubs with his tiny Japanese camera. After Velcroing the camera away in one of his pants pockets, he picked up his compass and held it level in his hand, orienting himself to the terrain. Once he'd exhausted his possibilities, he closed his eyes and was soon snoring lightly, his hand still gripping the Zippo lighter. He seemed at peace with the world.

We arrived at Cu Chi by mid-afternoon. After surviving the first barrage of hawkers selling lighters and pens made from bullets and "I've Been to the Cu Chi Tunnels" T-shirts, we were herded to a dark, basement-smelling room where we watched a black and white video of B52s dropping bombs on women and children as they ran, hands over their heads, out of the movie's frame.

A voice, dark and heavy, rumbled from the speakers on the walls. "Cu Chi, the land of many gardens, peaceful all year round under shady trees...Then mercilessly, American bombers ruthlessly decided to kill this gentle piece of countryside...Like a crazy bunch of devils, they fired into women and children...The Americans wanted to turn Cu Chi into a dead land, but Cu Chi will never die." Before our eyes could adjust to the light, we were herded like slow-moving cows to the jungle paths, which had been thinned and cleared for tourists.

Hai showed us one of the original openings of the Cu Chi tunnels, a circle the size of a human head. The Vietnamese started building the long tunnel during the 1940s, Hai told us. By the end of the war, it was seventy-five meters long with an entire society living underground.

"The Japanese, we could do this too," Kitano whispered. He grabbed the loose skin of his stomach and squeezed it. "But now too soft."

"Here," said Hai, gesturing to the whole group, "is the place for you. We made the tunnel larger so you can experience it."

Kitano decided to rent one of the Cu Chi guerilla uniforms available to tourists for a more authentic tunnel experience. The uniform fit him perfectly.

"You look like the enemy," the Canadian said.

"I am the enemy." Kitano laughed in short gasping breaths.

Led by Hai, we walked through the tunnel door

down to the first level about ten feet below the surface. The room opened to a kitchen, bunkers, and a command room. Even though the tunnels had been enlarged and outfitted with electricity for the tourists, the strapping Dutch couple bowed out before we descended to the second level where the serpentine tunnels narrowed. We didn't have to crawl so much as crouch. Except for the lack of windows, I was surprised by how livable the tunnels seemed.

Creeping hunchbacked through the rooms, I imagined living as they did, months at a time without seeing daylight. During the day, they went about the business of living, just as people all over the world did, except their lives were underground, secret and unseen, Hai told us. The Vietnamese would tend the rice paddies by the stars, and this life of darkness and bombs and night farming soon became a routine among the chaos.

"And what else can you do when bombs are falling?" Hai continued. "You go underground and go on with your life and you wait until the bombs have stopped. Then you emerge, assess what has been lost, collect what remains, and you continue. Go on or not. Those were the choices."

Was that what it had been for my father—choosing to leave all that was dead to him in order to go on? The rooms were lit with bare bulbs wired along the dirt walls. Kitano took out a Maglite to examine the darker parts more carefully.

"You've got a torch," Jenna whispered in an excited voice. "I think I found something. Would you be keen to check it out?"

We crept into the shadows of the room and waited

until the others had left. The air was cool and thick, which I consumed in short, shallow breaths. Kitano wielded the flashlight like a small weapon. He had left his other talismans with his clothes when he put on the VC uniform.

Jenna touched my elbow and led us a few feet farther back. "Shine the torch here."

It was a tunnel, but one that had not been expanded for the tourists, not much larger than a rabbit's hole. We crouched around and peered in the opening. Kitano waved the light above the hole like a magic wand. The tunnel remained narrow, but ended a few feet below.

"There's another level," Jenna exclaimed as she clapped her hands together. The sound echoed around us.

Kitano placed the flashlight in my palm. "I'm going down. Give me the flashlight when I ask."

"I don't think you should." I smoothed my hand over the photo and postcard in my pocket. The world was dangerous without the protection of talismans.

He looked at Jenna. "I will go." Kitano, like me, wanted to impress Jenna, and in the manner of someone who was used to having people try to impress her, she was letting him.

"Be careful." She touched the collar of his uniform.

Kitano was a small man. He held his arms up and folded his shoulders in. His head was level with the ground now. I shined the flashlight on what remained of him. He looked like a decapitated VC soldier. His eyes were closed and his face had a distant, serene expression. Jenna took off her bandana and knotted it around his forehead.

"Think of the Vietnamese who lived here. Go on.

Or not," I said.

Kitano disappeared down the hole.

"Brilliant," Jenna called down.

"You okay?" I waved the flashlight around the empty floor below.

"Give me light!"

"When I count to three," I said. "One, two, three." The flashlight thudded into the darkness. Time slowed with each breath. I felt as if I'd been born there.

The way I imagined it was this. While the others on his boat are getting their necks slit with wire, my father is passed out on a bag of rice in the storeroom below. He awakes with his mouth and eyes painfully dry. Outlines of rice bags, storage boxes, and bamboo baskets float around him. He grabs on to the silence, thick under the night jungle noises, sits with it, heavy and shapeless in his hands. The silence takes him to a place empty and permanently changing, a place without water or trees or sky.

"What do you see?" called Jenna.

"Oh my God!" Kitano's voice echoed beneath us.

"What?"

Kitano screamed, and then yelled in Japanese. The light shone back up at us, but we couldn't see his face. He shouted more Japanese.

"English, English," I yelled back.

"Help me. Up! Up!"

"Bloody hell." Jenna stuck her hands and then her head in the hole. "Grab my hands." She was a big-boned girl and taller than Kitano. "Hold on to me so I don't fall in," she said in a take-charge voice. I grabbed her waist. If I let go, couldn't hold her tight enough, she would disappear with him. What would I do then, stay and try to save them, or run and get help? I wasn't sure. Kitano was speaking Japanese again in rapid, agonized bursts.

"I got him." She pulled him up slowly, with effort, like a woman in reverse labor. When Kitano's head appeared, it was streaked with dirt and sweat. He collapsed on the ground like a forgotten child. The flashlight and bandana were gone. "Hush now," she whispered as she slowly stroked his head. His eyes were squeezed shut, and his lips murmured his native tongue.

"What was it like down there?" I tugged the sleeve of his rented uniform. "Tell me! What did you see?" Kitano shook his head. I inched my face closer to his. His eyes were open now, shifting like moving targets. "I have to know."

Kitano swallowed as Jenna dabbed his moist forehead with her fingertips. "My grandfather. He was hero too. Except we lost. He always tell me, 'Some things you never talk about.' I think that is good advice." He was panting again and his eyes were still now, looking at me with a newly discovered hatred. Jenna wrapped her arm around him as if she were shielding him from me, the enemy.

"You're okay," she whispered. "That's all that matters now. That's all that matters."

We arrived at the last part of our tour, the Mekong Delta, as the sun began to set. Hai led us down the embankment where the water reddened under the descending sun's glow. On the edge of the river, the thick shrubs darkened until they softly blended into the sky. A wooden boat sprouted fishing poles that arced then lost themselves in the water. A tethered raft covered in netting bobbed next to the small shack that was someone's home. The night insects were a symphony of chirps and hums that accompanied the painting in progress. I put my hand on my stomach. None of the movies or postcards were like this moment, this image so full and singing that I fell into empty quietness. Nothing had prepared me for the beauty of the place.

My own father must have missed it at first, that nostalgic beauty of home. I imagined him on the boat late in the afternoon talking with guys with names like Hank and Johnny. Hank, he would have been from the backwoods of Mississippi, Johnny from a place like Colorado. God's country, Johnny would call it. And then my father, he would talk about Virginia. Its wild blackberries, honeysuckles, and whippoorwills. Its spring flowers, azaleas, crepe myrtles, magnolias, dogwoods. The cardinals, robins, and bluebirds that built nests in his backyard. Then when he got back to Virginia all he could think about was the boiling sun sinking over the fishing lines that attached sky to water to land.

"You won't find it here," Hai whispered behind my shoulder. "Down the road, maybe. People there live the same as before the war, before the French even. You might want to go there. You won't find what you are looking for, but you might find something else."

The night hummed with the unfamiliar cries of exotic birds and insects. I followed a dirt path, dim and rocky in front of me. In the distance was a figure shimmering in white. We stopped a few feet from each other, like two wary animals unsure if they have met friend or foe.

She was a young girl, like I had once been, although I hoped she had parents waiting for her inside one of those lit houses. Behind her was a small cluster of huts, calm and quiet. I stepped toward her. She didn't move.

She wore white calf-length pants and a high-collared shirt like the schoolgirls on the bicycles. Her hair was pulled back and she was slight like the other Vietnamese. Her gaze was not unkind. She reached her hand out; it glowed under the darkening sky. I laced the small, delicate fingers with my own calloused hand.

She led me away from the river, away from the lights of the village, with only her dress to keep me from falling into that place that held all that we are told not to speak of. The girl pointed to the sky, and with her slim, graceful finger traced the circle of the sudden moon. The moon illuminated the others down on the embankment, a million miles away. A fisherman waved, his hand a pale silhouette under his boat's kerosene lamp. I abandoned the girl's hand and retraced my steps to join them.

I fell into the group just as the fishermen paddled the boat to shore. Hai motioned for us to follow. We were boosted by the driver's laced hands on board. Up close, the men looked older with their missing teeth and creased faces. Their pants, rolled unevenly and splattered with mud, grazed their skinned knees. Once in the boat, wedged between Hai and Kitano, I could smell salt and rotting wood along with the caught fish. The men passed around metal plates topped with grilled catfish, which we ate with our hands. One of the girls distributed sheets of moist towelettes she had stowed in her backpack for such occasions.

"Too many bones," a Dutch girl whispered. I made a point of foregoing the towelettes and ate the fish like the men did, taking the half-chewed bones out of my mouth and throwing them into the water. One man, unshaven with matted hair, brought out a bottle of homemade Mekong whisky from his pocket.

"The real stuff," said the Canadian.

"Brilliant," Jenna said. She had taken off her bandana to tie her hair back in a loose ponytail. She clinked glasses with the Canadian and the Dutch couple sitting next to her.

After we'd cleaned the bones of the fish, the fishermen passed around smudged glasses brimmed with Mekong whisky. Soon the group would be restless, cramped on this small boat, the experience having run its course. Later, in the safety of the darkened, windowless bar and their own kind, they would tell their tales about drinking Mekong whisky on a villager's boat. I felt contempt for their pitiful adventures, and yet envied them, those whose lives seemed unimpeded by loss.

Kitano held up his compass. "We are northwest of Saigon." His face was red from drinking twice as fast as the rest of us. He had not spoken to me since the tunnels. "This is like old way in Japan. Long ago we were same as here."

Hai smiled thinly. I was sure that to him, the old Japanese colonialists were no different than the French or the Americans. His scar was hidden in the night but he looked tired, and his eyes were somewhere else.

I wanted to tell the story of my father to someone.

Someone who would be impressed, someone still naïve, who believed in the magic of moons and mushrooms, someone who would believe me. Kitano was busy using his own talismans to exorcise whatever had happened in the hole. *Some things you never talk about.*

There was Hai. I was close enough to whisper everything in his ear. But he knew the truth, knew it better than I ever would. After a few shots of whisky, I shifted away from Hai and Kitano and squeezed in next to Jenna at the edge of the boat. I thought we might be friends now, after our time in the tunnel.

"I know a place where you can drink snake's blood," I said.

"So?" She looked away, to show me how unimpressed she was.

"My father was on this river during the war," I breathed into her ear.

"Really?" Even in the darkness I felt her scrutinizing me. This was my chance.

"One evening he gets high with some of the guys and goes down into the storage room and passes out on a bag of rice. When he wakes up, it's night. Everything is quiet, too quiet. He slowly opens the door to the deck."

Jenna set her glass down. Her shoulder touched mine. Her eyes were white and animal-like. "Then?"

"At first he only sees the shapes, outlines of forms. Then he makes out their necks and the blood from where the knives slit them. His voice cracks when he calls out their names, Hank, Johnny, George."

"Really?"

"It's true," I said, my voice tight. And for the most part, it was.

She breathed warm whisky on my neck. "Okay

then. What next?"

"He comes back home. I'm born. But me and my mother, we're not enough. So he leaves us for Thailand." That was not what I had planned to say.

"Big deal." Jenna drained her whisky and set the empty glass beside me. She turned away, a ghost receding into shadow.

My stomach hurt. I pushed myself up.

"I have to go," I said to the night air. One of the fishermen helped me onto shore. I was breathing heavily and my legs could not get a foothold on the embankment as I tried to climb up. I wanted to find the girl again. I wanted to show her the photo of my father and the postcard of the girls on bicycles. I wanted to tell her that her moon was more beautiful than mine. I wanted to grab her hand and tell her that it was a big fucking deal.

The dirt loosened under my grip, and I slid back down to the bottom. Closing my eyes, I heard Jenna's voice then, far away, back with the others, beginning another story about the moon. I raised my hand for her to lift me up.

She was calling my name, I was sure of it.

PICTURING SNAKES

After spending the morning stepping over bones and scraps of clothes that poked out of the grounds of the Killing Fields, Elise was happy to accept Arun's invitation to his house for lunch. Even as she traced her transparent reflection in the glass *stupa* stuffed with more than eight thousand skulls (classified by age and gender), the rumbling of her stomach had been an embarrassing reminder that although she was here to understand why people, and by extension herself, had suffered unfairly, her base human needs—food, shelter, clothing—demanded to be met.

Arun was waiting for her at his scooter, polishing the plastic and chrome with a blue bandana. He held the scooter steady for her to climb on.

"How far to your house?" Elise placed her sandals on the tiny metal extensions at the scooter's base.

"Not far," he answered vaguely. He climbed on the bike, allowed her a moment to circle her hands around him.

"What did you do before you were a driver?"

"After the Khmer Rouge, I was an orphan," Arun said. "I sold postcards."

"My parents are dead, too," Elise said.

"They were very old?"

"My father died when I was young. My mother almost two years ago."

"In America? How can that be? Your country is rich and powerful."

"Your country was rich and powerful once."

"Long time ago." Arun searched the sky then the ground as if the answer might be written there. "Shit happens, as you Americans say." He started the scooter. "Time to eat. You must be hungry."

The road to Arun's house was little more than a one-lane clearing with dust and rocks and crater-sized holes. Elise knew that walking would have been faster and more comfortable, but instead she tightened her hold on Arun's waist and closed her eyes to keep the dust from blinding her.

He wore a robin's egg blue, long-sleeve button-down shirt with a polo player sewn on the front pocket, the collar and cuffs frayed to a dingy white. Yesterday, when Elise first saw him wiping his already shiny scooter in front of the guest house she was checking into, he was wearing the same shirt. That night he had taken her to the Silver Pagoda, a glittering and majestic monument that mocked the poverty around them.

She guessed he would be wearing that shirt again

the next morning. He was to take her to the boat she would ride down the Tongle Sap River to Siem Reap, which housed the temples of Angkor Wat. He had already warned her that those boats were not safe and might capsize from being overloaded. He suggested that she fly instead, that he knew of someone who could sell her a ticket. She told him she would take her chances with the boat.

The scooter sputtered to a stop in front of a group of women and children gathered around an ancient TV. The TV was housed under a rickety wood and tin structure stacked with bottles of soft drinks and faded canned goods. The women were wrapped in *sarongs*, their ebony hair coiled low on their necks. They touched their children's shoulders who then ran toward Elise with their eyes large and palms open. She took a stack of *riels* out of her money pouch and passed out single bills, worth only a few cents.

"Dollar, please," one of the oldest demanded, holding out her hand. As soon as Elise shook her head and tucked the *riels* in her pouch, they ran back to the TV, their arms raised with their bills tight in their fists.

Arun led her along a dirt pathway past a row of simple bamboo and concrete homes. He stopped in front of a square building where a young woman was scooping water out of the well in front of their house. She, too, wore a *sarong* and was as beautiful as the other young Cambodian women Elise had seen. Also outside was a concrete stove and grill, where two large pots and a cluster of small fish hissed from the fire crackling underneath. After they greeted each other with a few soft words, Arun's wife went back to the stove, and he gestured for Elise to follow him inside.

The room was dark and cool and suddenly still. Arun unbuttoned his shirt and hung it on a nail jutting out of the wall next to a white shirt identical in cut. A small infant boy, naked and curled, slept on a straw mat while a young girl fanned his face. Although the girl's eyes were downcast, Elise could feel the girl's focus was on her. Arun's wife entered and turned on an electric fan plugged into an extension cord that ran out of the house to a generator.   He showed Elise the two framed pictures resting on a plank of wood that sat atop a pile of stacked stones. One was of him, his wife, and their infant son. The three of them, solemnly huddled into the center of the frame, looked more like siblings than parents and child. Elise smoothed her hand over her back pocket, where she kept the half photo of her father taken not long before he'd died.

The other picture was of Arun and an older western man with reddish hair and a large stomach that made him look pregnant. "He is my German friend. He paid for this house. Five hundred dollars."

Elise surveyed the concrete square dwelling, admiring its compact utility. "It's nice."

Arun shrugged. "It is enough for us." He said something to the girl, but she didn't look up or change the rhythm of her fanning.

"That's my niece. She lives with us. I pay for her school."

"That's kind of you."

"If I don't pay she can't go."

Arun's wife came in with plates of rice, broiled fish, sprigs of green plants, and sliced limes. The fish were small, and Elise picked the bones with the tines of her fork, while Arun ate his fish whole.

The wife lifted the baby and pressed him to her chest while she watched them eat. Arun and his wife spoke to each other in low even tones, without rancor or hostility, and Elise felt calmed by the steady, quiet rhythm. She wondered if they had reached a place of peace or just necessary detachment, borne out of unbearable loss and suffering.

After thanking them for the meal, she took a photo of the family with her camera, promising to send a copy to the guesthouse for Arun to pick up sometime in the unknown future.

Next was the Genocide Museum, a secondary school building converted into a place of torture under Pol Pot's regime. Now tourists could walk through the concrete rooms adorned only with the vestiges of that past—bare mattresses on metal springs, dried blood stained on the floors, electric prods, chains, and whips hanging from bare walls. Between the torture instruments hung black-and white framed photographs of the victims, their bodies electrocuted until they were only charred outlines on stained beds. Most of the posted explanations were in Khmer only, for reasons unclear to Elise. Few Cambodians could afford the one-dollar admission fee, and besides, Elise thought, why would they pay to see something they had lived? When she had offered to pay for Arun to come into the museum, he refused, saying he had seen it all before, but that he hadn't been to Angkor Wat yet, and hoped to do that someday.

It was the sparseness of the place, the lack of detailed explanations, the bloodstains, the torture implements ready for use that felt to her this had all happened yesterday and would again tomorrow. One wall of the museum was lined with hundreds of photos of the victims, headshots of them before their death, like a high school yearbook where the photographer had forgotten to remind them to smile. Another wall was populated with victims' skulls that mapped the shape of Cambodia.

Outside, the sun was strong, and Elise walked by the children tossing a volleyball toward Arun, who was wiping his scooter with a folded handkerchief. By the time she reached the scooter, the children had surrounded them again. They ran in packs, barefoot and in tattered clothes, some asking for candy or money, others selling postcards. The older ones edged their way up front, spreading the pictures of the temples at Angkor Wat like pages from a catalogue.

"Ma'am, you buy postcard."

"Just one." She chose a picture of a houseboat on the Siem Reap and paid for it. More children had gathered now, dropping postcards on her lap, surrounding her with pictures of the ancient Khmer temples. She shook her head and refused to meet their eyes. She hoped Arun would shoo them away, but he did nothing. Finally he started the scooter, and the children dispersed as quickly as they had gathered.

TALISMANS

Through the window near her table at the Foreign Correspondent's Club, Elise watched the people on the street below crawling, squatting, weaving, and strolling. Some balanced baskets on their heads, while others cradled children or guns with their free hands.

"Best sunset in Asia."

A clean-cut man in his early thirties with an American accent was standing next to her.

"No more seats," he said, sitting at her table. "Hope you don't mind."

"Not at all," she said before taking a sip of her gin and tonic.

He waved to the bar, and a young Asian man in dreadlocks and a Bob Marley T-shirt walked over with two Angkor beers and set them on the table.

"This is Haruki. I'm William." They raised their beers expectantly until Elise clinked her drink with theirs. They then took long draws, tipping the bottoms toward the ceiling. William said something in Japanese to Haruki, and the two laughed.

"First time here?"

Elise nodded. "I got in last night."

"Thought I hadn't seen you here before," William said.

A Rolling Stones' CD blared from speakers on the ceiling. A few men in trousers and button-down shirts sat on the stools at the bar. The tables were full of tourists and well-to-do locals drinking bottled beers and mixed drinks. The bar had a faded, wood-paneled colonial look that made the place feel more decadent than it really was. Haruki took out a pack of Marlboros from his jeans pocket and gestured to Elise. She shook her head. He pulled a lighter out of the pack and lit his cigarette, turning his head away from William as he exhaled the smoke from his mouth.

"Haruki's been here for a few days. I'm taking him to Angkor tomorrow."

"I'm going tomorrow, too."

"Plane or boat?"

"Boat."

"Same here. Great way to travel. All that about the boats being dangerous is a bunch of shit. Don't believe the crap people will tell you about ambushes and drownings. Sure they overload the boats, but I'd say it's about as safe as anything else here."

"Are there snakes?"

"In the river?" William shrugged. "Sure, why not?"

If Cambodia had snakes, then certainly Thailand did as well. Perhaps a snake had bitten her father after he'd fallen in the Kwai River, and he had drowned accidentally after all.

William suddenly looked toward the door, as if he had seen someone he knew, but no one came over to the table. "I guess you went to the Killing Fields and the Genocide Museum today."

Elise nodded and tossed her drink back. The ice slammed against her teeth.

William shook his head. "Always tough the first time. Where you staying?"

Elise told him the name of her guesthouse.

"That's where the French stay. Expensive, too—

what, twelve dollars a night? Me and Haruki, we're at the Rainbow. A bit of a hole, but it's the place to be. Rooms five dollars, lots of grass, laid-back. For three months I've been living off of ramen and smoking dope in a hammock. It's a great life."

Haruki was silent, watching her through slitted eyes. He said something to William.

"He can't speak much English," William said. "How'd you get here?"

"I have a scooter and driver outside."

"How much you paying?"

"Five for the evening."

"Did he tell you it's not so safe for you to be riding around on a scooter this time of night? You're a sitting duck. I bet he didn't tell you because he wanted his five dollars."

"He's a good guy. And five dollars isn't so much."

"That's what he's counting on you to think." William glanced at Haruki, whose face was like steel. "Hey. We're going to the Heart in a few. Grass is free. Tell your driver to go home. We'll make sure you get back okay."

In the cab to the Heart of Darkness, they sped past the crumbling French colonial architecture, past wandering children and frail, squatting men, past young girls in short skirts and red lipstick, past young boys, handsome and lean, pointing their AK-47s at anything that moved.

She climbed the stairs to the bar, trying not to trip over the cripples maimed from land mines, the children in their torn, dirty clothes, everyone with their hands out.

The Heart of Darkness, run by an ex-Vietnam vet who had settled there with his Cambodian wife, was packed with expatriates: journalists, English teachers, NGOs, and backpackers who drank and smoked in fleeting camaraderie. A few older men with large shirts untucked over their spilling stomachs played pool, while miniskirted prostitutes vacantly appraised the surroundings. William pinched some leaves out of one of the wicker baskets on the bar and rolled a joint, nodding to the grunge rock blaring from the speakers.

"Smoke?"

He passed the joint to Elise, where she held it briefly before inhaling, remembering the first time she'd smoked pot—the summer she was fourteen. She'd gone to a hill to escape the funeral of the boy she'd secretly loved. A girl there, a classmate, had passed her joint to her, much like William did now.

Plastic snakes and spiders of different sizes and colors hung from the ceiling. William raised his hand and touched a green snake suspended above them so that it bounced and jiggled on its elastic strings.

"I guess they do have snakes in Cambodia. Scared?" William asked, looking pleased with himself.

"Not really," Elise said. She reached up and ran her hand along the length of the snake, which was as long as her arm.

The night started to blur. She thought of Arun at home with his wife and baby and wondered if he was at all worried about her out this late. She hoped he was.

The music was slowing. She watched Haruki laugh for an absurdly long time. William filled a glass pipe and passed it to her. She held the smoke in her lungs for as long as she could before she blew it out. She was overwhelmed by a sudden smell and taste of incense.

"You down with ope, right?" William asked.

Elise nodded, even though it was her first time smoking opium. She tried to regulate her breathing and stay relaxed. She stared at the snake above her.

Months after the funeral, she'd been in a boat with another boy, although this one she hadn't loved, secretly or not. He rowed them across a lake until they were shaded in leaves and hanging branches. After they'd shared a beer, he'd leaned over and touched her lips and breasts at the same time just as a snake fell from the branch above them. Its black body slapped on the hot metal of the boat while its tongue shot darts at her. Terrified, she'd jumped in the water, and she felt then like she did now, both light and heavy, bright and dark, hot and cold, all at once. She wasn't sure if she would ever come up. When she was underwater, she saw her father there too, except that he was flailing, fighting to breathe. Then she felt a grip around her waist, and she was being pulled upward to air and sun and into the boat. She never forgave the boy for saving her.

William and Haruki sparkled near her, while the other objects faded into silhouettes. She was floating across the room now finding her way by touch.

She wanted to tell someone to turn down the music, but she had forgotten how to speak. She wanted to touch the greenish glow above her, but her arms were too heavy to move.

While her body had betrayed her, her mind was clear and unimpeded. She recalled math problems from high school that she had been unable to solve but whose solutions were now obvious. The music resonated around the room; its notes were reflected in the shadows of others in a profound way that she could not articulate. She picked out the individual harmonies and rhythms and followed them to their logical conclusion. She closed her eyes and bobbed her head with the music, so beautiful, so poignant, and then she was a girl again, wrapped in her bed listening to her mother play the most beautiful Beethoven. The soundtrack of her dreams. Now she was in one of those dreams and she could not stop smiling.

Things were making sense. Like that ubiquitous bumper sticker back in the States that Arun had quoted: shit happens. She laughed, fleetingly enlightened.

She commanded her arm to take the photo of her father out of her shorts pocket. Her father was soft and glowing. She had not seen it before. That her father was sending her a message through the photo. He was smiling right at her. She smiled back at him. She kissed the photo, then William, then Haruki, then the snake.

When she opened her eyes, the sun was out, and she was in her bed, alone.

The boat rumbled fast and loud down the river. William and Haruki were crashed out on their backpacks down below. Elise sat on the deck wearing a beige boat hat and sunglasses in an attempt to shield her face from the heartless sun. She felt raw and headachy. A few girls in bikini tops and short-shorts were sunning themselves on the corrugated roof, eyes closed, ears stuffed with Walkman earphones. The boat sped past the bamboo houses on stilts, fishing boats docked on the grass, and children splashing in the water.

What would happen if she walked over to the edge of this boat and jumped off as it sped by the bamboo huts, small dots along the river's edge? Would someone save her? Would she swim back? Would she let herself drown, just so she could feel what her father had?

She unzipped her money pouch and extracted the picture of her father. Palming the photo in her left hand, she traced its rough edges with her index finger. With his long hair and bandanna, her father looked carefree. The liquor bottle in his hand added to his enjoyment, just as the woman cut out of the photo must have.

She circled her father's face and trailed his smile, a soft curl like Arun's sleeping child. Last night had shown her: there were other ways to understand him.

That evening, Elise sat with William and Haruki on one of the hills to watch the sun set over Angkor Wat. They had met another backpacker on the way up, a Canadian woman with unshaven legs and underarms who wore multiple nose and tongue rings. The four passed a joint around in silence as they watched the sandstone temples turn copper then deep red under the darkening sky.

"I just don't understand," the Canadian girl said. "How can the same people do both? Make these monuments of incredible awe and beauty and yet kill their own by the millions?"

"Lots of slave labor for both projects." William spoke in Japanese to Haruki, and they laughed.

"I'm serious," the girl said.

"I am, too. You've got to think about the big picture." William drew an expansive frame with his fingers, then patted Haruki's leg. "Look at the Japanese. They were enlightened once. Then they got the brilliant idea to conquer the world. Got fried to a crisp for their effort."

"What the hell are you saying?" The girl's voice was tight and high-pitched.

Elise's mouth worked into a slow smile. "Shit happens. And then you die."

William laughed for a long time at that one. Haruki did, too. There was no need for translation.

And even though Elise laughed with them, she was thinking of when she would return on the boat in five more days. How Arun in his worn blue shirt would be waiting for her. How after that she would go to Thailand, where it was easy to get opium. How she would pass her days in a boat on the Kwai River. There, with only the moon and stars and sky to save her, she'd row to her father's ghost, the heart of her own ruinous peril.

BLUE

She prays that the dogs are sleeping and not dead. From the window of her floating bungalow, Elise watches them lying motionless on the deck, mottled strays hooked between the empty Singha beer bottles, greasy pad Thai cartons, and fried egg roll containers. The morning air clings to last night's revelations etched in urine and sewage. Beyond that, the Kwai River gently slaps the old tin boat tied to the dock. The river laughs at her.

According to her night visions and the half photo in her back shorts pocket, that river was where her father drowned almost twenty-five years ago, before she was old enough to remember him.

She turns from the window and falls back into bed. The ceiling is pale blue, her favorite color. Not for the reasons most people give—that blue is the color of sky, of water, of the person who no longer loves you. For her it is because her father painted her room blue before she was born.

Her bungalow rocks gently on thatched bamboo stalks cut from the jungle on the other side of the river. When Elise was a girl, her mother used to pull the bed sheet to her chin as if wrapping her up and sending her down the river like baby Moses. Then she would float endlessly in the dusk of the blue room, carried by the Beethoven her mother played on the piano in the living room. Elise pretended that each note was for her.

Yesterday she took a riverboat tour of the Buddhist caves with five other tourists: two French women, a Swiss couple, and Suzie from New Zealand. Elise sat next to Suzie, whose tan, boyish body was highlighted by a pink tank top and a purple batik *sarong*.

Elise was feeling warm from the opium she'd smoked before the boat trip. Below her, fish and snakes swam in figure eights. A voice broke through the water's bubbles. Words, circled in shiny iridescence, floated skyward until they popped. Then the words fell apart, each letter a rainbow fish diving into the water. The letters rose again, combining to form new sounds of a language that just exceeded her grasp.

The voice was bright, like a lightning bolt.

"You," it said. "Weren't you on a raft in Chiang Mai? We were starting the trip, you were finishing. We bumped rafts, remember?"

For Elise that raft trip had been hazy. The night before she had been in another world.

"Sure, I remember." The river's waves reached the boat like the hands of a drowning person.

"Pretty amazing, wasn't it?" the voice asked.

"Sure. Yes."

The November sun, young and glaring after the rainy season, burned a halo onto Suzie's short, razored hair.

Elise closed her eyes. Her father often came to her when she smoked. This time he was about seven or eight, fishing with his own father on a lake near his house in Virginia. She was near him in another boat, fourteen again, with a boy her own age who was searching for dark spaces so that no one could find them. Because her father could not travel through space and time, he did not see Elise watching him through the yellow- and red-veined hands of the autumn trees. She was surprised that as a boy her father had a cowlick, dark and untamed.

Her father plucked a worm from a tin can packed with earth and pierced his fishing hook. He caught one fish, her grandfather, three. The fish her father caught slapped against the ice in the cooler. While her grandfather smoked a cigarette, her father grabbed the fish, its silvery scales cutting into his skin, and tossed it overboard.

A snake fell from a tree into their boat. Jumping into the lake, she followed the mist of blood from the fish her father had thrown back, its mouth choking on hooked worms. The boy fashioned the snake into a life preserver, which he then threw overboard for her to grab.

A bird's talons swooped in the water and picked Elise up by her shirt collar. Her hair tipped the edges of the river, murky from the rainy season that had just finished.

"What are you doing?" Suzie squawked.

"Chasing something. A snake or a fish."

Suzie clawed at the air and flashed her eyes, a cold blue that revealed her true nature.

"You could've fallen in." Suzie's halo spread until her body was a chakra of glowing white.

"*You* would have saved me."

When they arrived at the shore, the French women stopped to look at the wares, and Suzie wandered off to buy a Coke. Meanwhile, Elise wavered from stall to stall, showing the owners the half-photo of her father clinging to his whisky bottle with a heightened smile. The Thais held the image between thumb and forefinger, arm's length away, squinting at something they preferred not to remember. They shook their heads and returned the photo before it burned the skin from their hands.

As the tourists walked up the hill toward the cave, the crossing gate lowered for an approaching train. They stopped to admire the jade bracelets the French women had just bought, deep, cool stones set in gold. That was why none of them saw the sleeping dog until it was too late. Spread across the tracks, the dog must have been trapped in its visions, as Elise was in hers. Their breathing kept time with the pulse of the early afternoon sun. The train's whistle chimed a warning. The dog raised its flea-bitten head, dazed, then stood but didn't move, as if dulled by the heat and gripped by dreams. The engineer flashed a wide Thai smile of gold teeth that was as hospitable as it was inscrutable. When the train ran over the dog, the engineer's glinting mouth opened, and his head bobbed in unsuppressed mirth.

The car hit Elise's mother head-on as she turned left from the church parking lot onto the four-lane highway. Her head crashed through the windshield, which cut a constellation in her throat.

"*Mon dieu*," one of the French women said.

"Terrible!" cried the Swiss man.

The engineer laughed and waved. The train, only four cars long, churned past the now silent group, its wheels chugging with each revolution.

A speckled mess of open wounds and missing fur, the dog lay on the tracks a few seconds, then tried to push itself up, not realizing one leg was missing and the other was hanging by cords of tendon and muscle.

Suzie gasped. "It's still alive."

By now the locals had gathered. They were laughing quietly. The dog kept trying to push itself off the tracks, only to collapse back on the ground.

"Somebody do something!" Suzie squeezed Elise's arm.

"What?" Elise was laughing along with the Thais. She suddenly found the idea that someone could do something when confronted with death to be very funny. Elise winked at the locals and laughed harder.

In her mother's last moments, space and time had no longer existed. She had seen Elise's father, long-haired, sunburned, rowing while he sang Hank Williams' "I'm So Lonesome I Could Cry." Then she saw Elise, here, in the future, witnessing this very accident.

Elise watched her mother watching her. *Elise,* her mother whispered, *why are you living?* Her face was bloody and there were tubes so that she could breathe. She touched her index finger and thumb together. Elise tried to lift her hand toward her mother, but it was suddenly heavy and would not leave her side. The scent of blood coated her nostrils. *Elise,* her mother whispered again, *why are you living?*

"I've forgotten."

"What do you mean you've forgotten?" Suzie's voice was like a blade. "*I'll* never forget this. Not in a million years."

Other dogs circled around the stray who struggled

to stand. They seemed intent on watching it die.

Elise followed Suzie as she stumbled down the street back to the boat. Suzie climbed in and curled into a sob. Elise sat beside her.

"You laughed. With those bloody barbarians."

"We all have our ways of dealing with death." Elise felt calm and remote. She whispered in Suzie's ear. "I have something that will make you feel better."

"What could *you* have for me?" Suzie asked, not unlike a child. She wiped her eyes and would not look at her.

"Magic. And the power that goes with it."

That night, Elise met Suzie on the dock, her face splotched from crying. She felt better after a few hits, though, and was easing her way into forgiveness. They sat on the dock and listened to the jungle across the river. Birds, monkeys, and secret animals communicated in pitches perfect and distinguished in their own way. That the wild had its own rhythms was comforting.

"You hear it?" Elise pointed to the old tin boat a few feet away, tied loosely to the dock.

"I hear the water." Suzie leaned back and arched her neck. "It's saying, 'okay, okay, okay.'"

"No, it's the boat." Elise rubbed her hands on the splintered boards. "It's saying, 'come in, come in, come in.'"

"Okay, okay, okay." Suzie shook her head, which was tilted toward the guesthouse restaurant behind them.

Elise touched Suzie's hand. "Let's go."

Suzie lurched forward, still shaking her head, then pushed herself to standing. "Not again. I'm not going there. Not when I'm feeling magical. Not when there are boys up there." She turned toward the restaurant, where tables of young men from all around the world, lean and shirtless, were drinking Thai whisky.

"Don't follow me," she called as she faded into the night.

"Not planning on it," Elise yelled. Then in a whisper: "You'll be back."

The clouds cleared to reveal a moon swollen with promise. Elise climbed in the boat, untied the rope and paddled eastward.

The night her father had drowned he was chasing the moon. He had learned how to navigate by the moon from his own father. If the moon rose before midnight, then the lit side was west. If the moon rose after midnight, then the lit side was east. He was drunk and he had forgotten what his father had taught him. It was after midnight and he thought he was paddling west. He paddled away from his house, away from his Thai wife, until he was lost. With the moon's reflection in the water, he reached out to touch it, thinking that he was going home. He grabbed at the moon and it disappeared, so he jumped in to chase it.

He bobbed a few times to the surface, too drunk to remember to breathe. He had forgotten he had arms and legs and he flapped his hands like they were gills. There was no one to save him.

Elise was back on shore to get help. She ran through the night market, the cut photo in her hand. When the villagers saw the photo, they thought the man was Jesus. They made a small fire and burned him, laughing as his face curled and melted in the flames and then rose as shapes in a sulfurous sky. The smoke signals sent Elise back to the river where, they told her, her father was still drowning.

She found herself flailing in the water, chained to

clumps of seaweed that kept her from reaching the surface. Then she saw him, not a bearded Jesus, but clean-shaven in shirt sleeves, the way he was before he left. Daddy. He disappeared into the murky moments of the river before she could ask him how he had learned to live without breathing.

The seaweed loosened its choke, and she scratched her way to the surface. Elise hurled herself back into the boat and sucked in perfect breaths, moist and round.

She paddled to the dock, illuminated by the moon. The animals on the other side sang in harmony, the sounds distinct yet unified. Standing on the dock, thin as bamboo, was Suzie, clutching a life preserver to her chest.

The next morning, Elise awoke under a canopy of mosquito netting next to Suzie, who was snoring lightly on her stomach. Elise put on her T-shirt and shorts and walked across the open yard to her floating bungalow.

Now, a few hours later, Elise lies in her bed on the water. She thinks of the dogs outside, wonders which ones are dead or just sleeping, and stares at the ceiling of endless blue.

There's a knock on her door, faint, more a question than a statement. She doesn't move.

"Elise, you there? It's Suzie. You must have left while I was asleep."

Blue is a lonely color for lonely people—cool, calm, yet remote. Her mother had cried when she walked into the house and smelled the sharp bite of fresh paint from Elise's bedroom. She thought it signaled Elise's father's return to them, not his goodbye.

Suzie knocks louder and faster.

"I just want to thank you for, well, you know, last

night. But even now I can hardly think about the dog without crying. The image, I can't lose it."

Elise examines her fingers. The tips are burnt from where she held the edge of her father's photo as it curled into smoke signals and disappeared into the night sky.

As her mother was dying, she had finally seen that Elise's father had awakened many mornings that month determined to paint his unborn child's room. That he finally did was a victory. That he was unable to sustain this victory, to build on it, did not take away from the glory of that moment. People forget that, Elise thinks. People like her mother, like her grandfather, like herself. Even people like Suzie.

Suzie's flip-flops slap down the dock to solid ground. She will come back, but by then Elise will be in some other room made of teak and bamboo with broad-leaved banana trees outside her window. There, she will wrap herself in her memories, fearlessly, in time and space, without the opium, without the blue.

Outside, the dogs are waking, one by one by one.

THE ICE
QUEEN

I met Tommy, my pretend husband from Canada, on a day when I'd almost thrown myself into Bangkok's Chao Phraya River. Still weak from quitting my opium habit, I was riding a water taxi around the city with no real destination, leaning farther and farther over the thin, wobbly railing that lined the boat. The railing was an insufficient restraint against my own body, which was willing itself to fall accidentally. I doubled over and inhaled the warm dankness of a river long polluted with cigarettes and Styrofoam. I was ready to succumb to whatever was below. But some invisible force held me back, and instead of falling in the water, I dry-heaved into the open air.

I got off at the next stop and sat on the edge of the dusty pier, waiting for the world to settle. That was when Tommy appeared, tall, dark blond, and pale, offering me a lukewarm Coke in a glass bottle. The Coke tasted flat, but at least I was able to keep it down. He sat beside me and stretched his long legs across the dirt and broken glass. He was wearing the ubiquitous beige drawstring rayon pants on offer at backpacker stalls that dotted the tourist parts of the city.

"How long have you been traveling?" he asked. He leaned against one of the wooden posts on the pier. He was big-boned, with a wide rib cage and strong thighs. Later, whenever we had sex, which was usually twice a week, I felt trapped for air under his lumbering bulk.

"About a year." I dangled my flip-flops inches above the plastic and white foam undulating in the river's water.

"Me too!" He swallowed and moved his lips like he was blowing bubbles, which I later found out meant he was excited or agitated. "So far I've seen Angkor Wat in Cambodia, Borobudur in Indonesia, the Great Wall of China, Ayutthaya in Thailand, and India's Taj Mahal." He laughed apologetically. "Planned and saved for it since I was a kid. The only place that's left is Bangan, the land of a thousand temples. After Bangan, back to good ol' Canada." He spread his legs wider and leaned back on his elbows, claiming the space around him the way westerners often did, territorially, without thinking. "You from Canada?"

"States."

"Ah," he said, as if that explained something. "Where you headed?"

"Not sure." I drained the Coke and rolled the bottle in my hands. Those days, I was fighting my way back to the world of the living a minute at a time.

"I'm still deciding between Vancouver and Toronto," he continued, as if I had been the one who had asked the question. "When I get back, I'm going to have a T-shirt made—Wonders of the World: Asia—like those concert tour shirts, except this one would list the places

I've been and the dates. Pretty cool, eh?"

I nodded. Tommy leaned in. "I'm going to *use* all this wisdom I've gotten from this trip and do something with my own life that's great and enduring."

"Like this Coke bottle?" I raised the empty bottle so the glass refracted the sun.

"Ha-ha. You Americans, always so sarcastic." He swallowed and bobbed his head. "You don't seem in such good shape." He considered me for a moment. "You need a plan."

"Any ideas?"

Tommy swallowed excitedly. He took the Coke bottle and rubbed it like it was a genie's lantern. "I think I have just the thing."

A month later, in Myanmar (although Tommy insisted on calling the country by its former, more politically correct name, Burma), we had come to the end of our self-guided tour of the Shwedagon Pagoda in Rangoon. All I could think about was going back to our hotel room and taking a nap. The dizzying array of jeweled temples, backlit *stupas*, and reticent Buddhas swathed in a thin sheet of gold had tired me out.

I pointed to a banyan tree and told Tommy I'd wait for him there while he bought watermelon slices from a girl selling them from a tray perfectly balanced on the center of her head.

I rested against the wide trunk, which, according to the tree's sign, had grown from a branch of the banyan the Buddha had sat under when he became enlightened. Soon, I was asleep.

I awoke to Tommy tapping my shoulder. He was sitting next to me, cross-legged, and his lips were moving like a fish under water. He handed me a slice of watermelon, and I bit into its watery sweetness.

"Want to see tomorrow's plan?" He held the *Lonely Planet* open and directed my eyes to the yellow Post-It note two thirds of the way down. It was stuck next to a place on the map called Mrauk U. Tommy spent a good portion of each day highlighting the important parts of the *Lonely Planet* and color-coding them with matching Post-It notes cross-referenced with *The Rough Guide*. He was quick to tell anyone who would listen that while *The Rough Guide* contained more detailed cultural explanations, the *Lonely Planet* boasted superior maps. Therefore, it was imperative to own both books.

"Here." He leaned in and creased the book open. I closed my eyes and savored the watermelon seeds I'd pocketed in my cheek. He began reading.

"*Hidden in the encroaching jungle, in hill country close to the Bangladesh border, Mrauk U is reached only by riverboat—well off the beaten track! It is noteworthy for its Arakanese art and architecture, and its Buddhist temple ruins. Mrauk U is accessible from Sittwe in western Myanmar.*"

"But I thought we came here to go to Bangan." I spit the seeds into the palm of my hand, then planted them into the dirt at the tree's base.

"That's the grand finale, the *piece de resistance.*" He said the last words in an exaggerated French accent. "What do you think?" His hand lightly stroked my knee through the fabric of my cotton skirt, which was his way of reminding me that we were scheduled to have sex that night.

After we first agreed to the pretend marriage, Tommy explained to me that he didn't have a lot of time for sex these days since he would probably be in Asia only once and had a schedule to keep. There was more to see than he had time for, while sex, as great as it was, he assured me, could be indulged in back home, where there wasn't as much to see or do.

I brought my hand up to cover my yawn. Through the fog of my nap, the golden *stupas* had a surreal, theme-park look to them. "Sure, whatever. It's your call."

The next morning, while our driver took us through paved and dusty two-lane roads to the airport, Tommy reviewed his notes. I watched the Burmese, striking in their *longhis* and cotton skirts the colors of wet earth and washed-out skies. Most of them were focused on the business a new day demanded: they rode their bikes, carried baskets on their heads, sold vegetables, bargained, prayed, laughed. I was struck once again by how life, no matter where it was in the world, carried on. A trite revelation, but a comforting one in its solid indisputability.

We boarded a small plane to Sittwe and then got a ride to the pier where we were to board a boat to Mrauk U, all prearranged by the only independent tourist agency in Sittwe, called Max Sunshine Tours. While we waited for our boat, another westerner emerged from a hired car, a compact man, tan with light-brown hair, smoking a cigarette. As soon as he saw us, he strode over and asked if we had a boat yet. Tommy told him we were paying eighty dollars for the boat, roundtrip—about three month's wages of the average Burmese.

"I'll pay a third if you don't mind me tagging along," the man said in a slight German accent. "I'm Konner." He gave us each his business card, which said he was a banker in Frankfurt. He looked to be in his mid-thirties, but youthful in the way a man does who has never married or experienced much tragedy. He wore freshly laundered jeans and a light denim cotton shirt the color of his eyes with the sleeves rolled to just below his elbows. His hair was cut short and sported a tidy but receding hairline.

As we continued to exchange pleasantries, a group of young boys emerged from the thatched houses nearby and crowded around us. Dark and barefoot in tattered shorts and T-shirts, they hung onto each other in easy camaraderie. They whispered and laughed good-naturedly, gazing at us like we were strange and exotic creatures, yet they did not approach us or spread their hands out for pencils or money.

"They're not jaded yet," Tommy said. "Not enough tourists here to spoil them."

"That's why I keep coming back," Konner said. "My fifth trip. There's none of the stealing or begging you get in the other Asian countries. Look." He walked over to the boys and squatted down so that he was at their eye level. The boys folded inward, but didn't run away. Konner pointed to a rubber ball the size of a baseball one of the older boys was holding.

"Nice," he said. "Good." He nodded.

The boy's eyes widened. Slowly he extended his hand and uncurled his fingers so that the ball lay open in his palm. Konner took the ball.

"Mine?"

The boy nodded slowly.

Konner grinned at us. Then he tossed the ball back to the boy. The boy's face scrunched up and I thought he might cry, whether because he had almost lost the ball or had gotten it back, I wasn't sure.

It was true that the Burmese, while being the poorest and most repressed people on a continent of poor and repressed people, seemed more intent on giving than receiving. So far there had been none of the desperate begging of the Cambodians or the relentless touting of the Vietnamese. I wasn't sure if the Burmese attitude came from the repressive regime, their devout Buddhism, years under British rule, or a combination of all three.

The boys followed us to the pier to see us off, and they waved goodbye as if we were relatives about to sail for the new world. The boat was a rickety, loud vessel, like most of the boats on the river. There was a storage space underneath that carried supplies to Mrauk U, and a small room that housed the engine, a toilet, and cooking facilities. The crew was composed of a captain, first mate, and a cook who served us curry and rice, the Burmese staple.

We sat in the open air under a tin roof, drinking tea and coffee while Konner smoked his Marlboro Reds. He and Tommy swapped traveling stories, their voices loud and strained above the din of the motor.

Tommy told Konner about the travel agency he used here, gleaned from the "Thanks" section of the *Lonely*

Planet, which fit into his theory about the travel book. He believed that the *Lonely Planet* was actually written on two levels. The surface reading was the straightforward one, which was intended for most readers.

"I don't share this with many people," Tommy said in a lowered voice, even though there was no one around to overhear, "but the deeper meaning is only for those astute enough to read between the lines."

While they talked, I contented myself with watching the families living along the water, their fishing boats tethered to wooden sticks, their nets secured along the bank, the women washing their clothes in the water. Two men herding a group of oxen waved from the riverbank.

"Of course the country is one of the most repressive in the world," Tommy said, as if Konner had challenged his reasons for being here. "A Nobel Prize winner under house arrest. Human rights violations left and right. Terrible. No doubt about it. But what about India, do people stop going there because of its caste system? Or China—do you really think China is much better with its treatment of the Tibetans? Or what about the U.S.? One of the worst violators of human rights in the world. Just ask Amnesty International."

"You must not be American, then." Konner smiled slyly.

"Canadian," Tommy said in a voice that Canadians used when they wanted to distance themselves from Americans. "My wife is, though. American."

I jerked my head up at the word "wife," and fingered my fake wedding ring, a thin silver band that matched Tommy's. We had bought them for ten dollars from one of the vendors selling jewelry on the street in Bangkok.

After our talk on the pier, Tommy had taken me back to his room at the guesthouse, a cramped particle-board box that was windowless but had AC, and told me about his fake marriage plan. He said that married western couples got much better treatment in Asia than singles or unmarried couples. Single men were untrustworthy because they might hit on the local women; single women were loose and without morals; couples living in sin were doing just that. He'd seen married couples, especially newlyweds, get rooms with bigger beds and better views, cheaper fares from the taxi drivers, and bigger portions and special treats from street vendors and family restaurant owners.

He'd been toying with the fake marriage idea for a while, but so far had not had any takers. No vision, he said. He could tell I was different, though, and would see the beauty of his plan. Since I had run out of options, I agreed to a trial run. We started pretending we were married in Bangkok, where it didn't really matter so much. It was just the kind of fantasy I needed for a while, something simple and crudely romantic despite its practical underpinnings.

Konner stared at me. His eyes were so light you could almost see through them. "How long have you been married?"

"One month," Tommy said, quickly. He draped his arm over the back of my chair, which was next to his. "Happiest month of my life. This trip is our honeymoon."

That was the first I'd heard of it. I decided then that Tommy probably made a better pretend husband than he would a real one.

TALISMANS

The boat pulled into the pier in Mrauk U a few hours past sunset. I first saw the regal woman then; she stood tall and motionless on the pier, like a statue posed for eternity. Her face and body were all bones and angles, the sharp yet smooth lines of a classic beauty. She wore a long red *longhi* and a loose gold short-sleeve top.

The woman on the pier said a few words into the sky and the people around her came to life. As we docked, they scrambled to the boat and helped the crew unload the baskets from storage below. Two plump and sullen women who looked to be in their thirties stood next to the older woman. They must have been her daughters, loyal and devoted.

The woman and I caught eyes. She nodded at me as if we shared a secret. I turned away.

A man in his late twenties with short hair, a wide face, and a missing tooth stooped over to help us out of the boat. "I'm Vinh, your driver."

"Are you with Max Sunshine?" Tommy asked.

"Yes. Max Sunshine," he said, then repeated himself as if he too were not used to the phrase, "I'm Vinh, your driver."

He helped us carry our bags to his car, a beat-up mid-eighties Chevrolet. Once we had settled in, he showed us a creased picture of two children, a boy and a girl about five and seven years old.

"Son. Daughter," he said, then re-taped the photo onto the dashboard.

"Your family, they depend on you," I said.

"Yes. I am good father, husband." Vinh straightened his back so that he looked taller. "I know place for you," he said. "Cheap. Five dollars."

"We'll look at it," Tommy said, "but no promises."

Two men around Vinh's age were at the table playing cards when we came into the Royal Palace. They jumped up and greeted Vinh with a flurry of conversation, then brought us up to the second floor and showed us the five small rooms with bunk beds covered in thin but clean sheets. Wire hangers hung from shiny nails. The showers and toilet were at the end of the hall, musty from the smell of wet concrete and rusty pipes.

"You like?" they asked with the excited urgency of someone who has put out their best finery for an important guest.

I was ready to stay and help Vinh and his extended family with their fledgling careers, but Konner would have none of it.

"I only get one month of vacation a year. I at least want my own bathroom."

Tommy nodded and we walked outside to the car where Vinh was waiting, smoking a cigarette. He wore jeans and a white T-shirt with blue writing in Burmese. I wondered if I could be with someone like Vinh, if he were single. Could I be his wife, have his children? Could we cross language, culture, race, education, income, everything that divides people in this world? It didn't seem likely.

Tommy slung off his backpack and extracted the *Lonely Planet*. "This looks nice," Tommy told Vinh, "but we'd like to go here." He pointed to the Max Sunshine Resort Hotel, highlighted in blue in the *Lonely Planet*.

"That place is full," Vinh said. "Here is good."

"Still, we want to go there," Tommy said, clearing his throat. He became quickly irritated if he thought he was being taken advantage of by the locals.

"If you don't take us, we'll get another driver," Konner said. He was small and compact with muscular forearms exposed under rolled-up sleeves. He smelled like cigarettes and aftershave, the way I imagined my father might have smelled when he came home from work.

Vinh, having no choice, silently drove us to the Max Sunshine Resort Hotel, which was crowded with older Europeans on package tours. They had the relaxed, clean look that only hot showers and planned itineraries can provide. Stretched out around teakwood tables, they sipped Carlsbergs and pink cocktails with matching paper umbrellas.

Tommy approached a man in a white button-down shirt who appeared to be the manager and asked him if there were any rooms. As Tommy spoke, the man shook his head, showing him a large book, then raising his hands to the sky.

"No room at the inn." Tommy shrugged. He hunched his shoulders and cleared his throat.

The guests, who had seemed pampered and staid before, now looked enticing and enviable. They clinked drinks and laughed throatily in their linen and silk, all under the attentive eyes of the Max Sunshine staff. We huddled outside the building in the dark, ignored or unnoticed by guests and staff. A few feet away from us, Vinh leaned against his car, smoking. Konner extracted a business card from his wallet.

"I'm not staying at that other place. This is my vacation." Konner strode toward the manager, tapped the registry book and made sweeping gestures around the rooms and restaurant as he talked. The regal woman from the pier suddenly emerged from some back room in the hotel with her daughters close behind. Her dark hair was threaded with silver and tied back to expose a graceful neck and high cheekbones. I was excited but not surprised to see her, the way people feel when an important figure appears at a time of crisis.

Konner presented his business card to the woman and talked in low, calm tones. The woman looked away while he was talking and saw me standing with Tommy. She nodded at me almost imperceptibly, and said something quickly to the manager before returning to the kitchen. The two women and the manager, faces lowered, scurried behind her. I too wanted to follow her as her daughters did, follow her to the ends of the earth.

Konner clapped us both on the shoulders and told us they had a room. "Thanks to a last-minute cancellation. I'm sure the room was always available, but the manager didn't want to be bothered with the extra work. After I talked to the owner, she arranged everything."

"That woman is the owner, then?" I asked.

"Yes, apparently. Most of these people you see working here are related to her. Must be a widow, the matriarch around here. You just have to know who has the power in places like these, then you can get things done." He seemed pleased to have dealt with a person at the top. "I told them that you were recently married, on your honeymoon, and wanted a nice place to stay. I hope you don't mind." He raised his eyebrows at me. His tone sounded slightly mocking, although Tommy didn't seem to notice.

"Not at all," Tommy said, giving me a knowing

glance. "Not at all."

"We'll have to share the room for the next few nights until another one is available. They'll set a cot up for me in the front part. Thirty dollars a night."

"Not a problem," Tommy said. "It *is* our honeymoon." He put his arm around me and hugged my shoulder to him. "See," he whispered in my ear. "Works like a charm every time."

Vinh nodded in a slow, defeated way when Tommy told him that we were staying here. Wordlessly, he hoisted our bags out of the trunk of his car. I wanted to take him aside then, tell him I was sorry I wasn't staying at his hotel helping him get a start in this world. He would nod in understanding and take me to his little hotel to live there indefinitely. I would pay for my room by cooking and cleaning, putting my pretend-wife skills to good use.

The Max Sunshine was a hotel that catered mostly to tour groups and its amenities reflected that. We had our bags carried to our room and were given wet washcloths to wipe our faces and watery orange juice as we completed the check-in process. Later, while we had curry and Myanmar beer outside on the terrace, the wait staff cooled us with fans that looked like palm leaves.

"It's okay. You can go," I said, waving the staff away.

"They really take this servant thing a bit too far," Tommy said. "Those Brits were amazing colonialists, really made the French and Dutch look like amateurs." Tommy said things like that, pretending he knew more about the world than he really did.

I was enjoying the beer, and, surprisingly, Konner's gaze that lingered a little too long on me, like he was still trying to decide what he wanted.

For the first time since before the opium, I wanted men. Their muscular forearms, the smell of sweat thinly disguised under deodorant and cologne, the bitten-down nails, the chapped spots in surprising places. I wanted Konner. I wanted Vinh. My skin tingled like it was sprouting new hairs.

We drank a few more beers, and then Tommy stood up, stretching his arms in an exaggerated yawn. "I'm ready for some shut-eye."

"I'm going to have another beer. Care to join me?" Konner raised his glass at me.

Tommy placed his hand on my back. I was tempted, but I had always gone to bed when Tommy did. And despite those bubbles of desire, each one shiny under its own light, I wasn't ready to let go of the one sure thing in my life.

"Another time." I drained my beer, and prepared myself for another night of efficient yet adequate sex.

The next morning we arranged for a car to take us to Wethali, to see the Great Image of Hey Tauna Pie, which Tommy had convinced us would be worth the two-hour trip. Even though Konner had been to Burma numerous times, this was his first time to Mrauk U, and he seemed as willing as I was to let Tommy do all the planning. Vinh waved to us from his car, wearing the same jeans and T-shirt as yesterday.

Vinh made up for his lack of English with

uncontrolled enthusiasm and a desire to please. He stopped the car often when he thought there was a tourist photo opportunity. This usually involved young girls skirted in their faded *longhis,* carrying water jugs on their heads. Tommy and Konner would take the requisite pictures, and then we'd continue on until the next oxen or water jug photo-op arose.

At one point Vinh stopped by a lotus pond. It was still early enough in the day for the flowers to be in bloom, saturating the world in their pinks and reds. Near the pond, Vinh showed us a plant that opened and then closed when touched, a small innocuous-looking green thing with leaves like miniature ferns. Tommy took a picture of me fingering the plant and another of it folding in on itself.

"I like your shirt," Konner said to Vinh as we walked back to the car. "I've been looking for a T-shirt with Burmese writing on it, but they all only have English on them. Do you know where I can buy a shirt like that?"

Vinh shook his head. "Very hard," he said.

We got into the car, Konner taking the front seat, Tommy and I the back. I was resting my head against the window when Vinh pulled his shirt over his head and tossed it to Konner. His body was even more beautiful than I'd imagined, brown and hairless, his stomach all muscle and skin, his shoulders broad and smooth. He reminded me of my South Korean boyfriend from over a year ago. "You can keep," he said.

"Thanks." Konner was already folding the T-shirt neatly and putting it in his backpack. He didn't even pretend to act surprised. "Here, have these." He placed two packs of Marlboro Reds on the dashboard next to the photo. Vinh caressed the cellophane but left the packs there, perhaps saving them to share with the guys I'd seen playing cards at the Royal Palace. I wasn't sure if I admired or hated Konner in that moment for his effortless manipulation.

"Givers, not takers, that's the Burmese for you," Tommy said, stretching his legs.

I wondered what it would be like to be Vinh's wife, to be the mother of his children. Would he be devoted and never leave me? I imagined how in the middle of the night he would take me in his arms and I would rub my hands over his skin, tanned and rough, the muscles hard and sinewy, his stomach flat as glass. And then something in me would melt, that *thing* that kept me numb, that kept me alive until I could live again. It would melt into a puddle. And when that puddle dried up, there would be a space, unfillable, permanent, a space that could hold things like grief and love and gratitude.

Wethali was a disappointment. We drove forty kilometers in two hours through rock-ridden dirt roads. The Buddha statue was supposed to be "the great image," from when the Wethali kingdom reigned from the third to tenth centuries, of which the kingdom of Mrauk U became the successor. The Buddha was tired and small, chipped and in need of paint and repair. I wondered why we'd spent the gorgeous day on bumpy roads just to see this.

"Well, its significance must be spiritual rather than artistic," Tommy said, as he and I quickly looped around. Konner smoked his Marlboro Reds with Vinh by the car, having taken one look at the statue then turned back. The return trip was spent in relative silence. I was suddenly tired and tried to sleep with my head against the door, but the car jostled me awake every time I neared the world of dreams and beyond.

ℌ

That night back at the Max Sunshine we ate lobster and drank Myanmar beer under a star-filled sky. Tommy had a full day planned for tomorrow, a morning car trip to a village outside Mrauk U and an afternoon of bicycle riding to nearby temples. After the third round of beers Tommy excused himself to go to bed since we had to be ready to leave at eight in the morning. As he stood up, Konner signaled the waiter.

"One more?" he asked me.

"Sure," I said, sinking back into my chair. The tingles were now vibrations. The new hairs were blossoming into flowers.

Tommy hovered for a second before leaning over and kissing me on the lips. "We got a long day tomorrow. Sure you don't want to come to bed?" Even though he was smiling I could feel the undercurrent of hostility in his voice.

"Just one more beer. I'll be back soon." I squeezed his hand. Konner ordered two more beers. Tommy nodded and walked back to the room, slowly, as if he were waiting for me to change my mind. He looked lonely then, and I almost jumped up and joined him. Instead I smiled at Konner as he filled our glasses.

"How long have you two been together?"

"About a month." I took a long drink.

"Beg your pardon? A month?" He put his beer down and shifted forward. He had changed into a crisp, blue shirt for dinner that was unbuttoned enough to reveal tufts of curly blond chest hair.

"Give or take."

"I'm confused. I thought you were married a month. Did you meet and get married on the same day?" He lit a cigarette and stared at me with narrowed eyes.

"Actually, we just pretend to be married to make traveling easier. Married couples get the royal treatment." I looked down at my beer. It hadn't sounded as silly when Tommy said it.

"You're not married?" He shook his head and whistled.

"Not even close. Tommy's all right, don't get me wrong, but I'd go crazy if I was married to him." I felt pleased at my unexpected betrayal.

He laughed. "I wondered how you could stand him all the time. He's a bit..." He paused as if searching for the word in English. Then he made a chopping motion across the table. "Rigid. More German than I am."

I laughed louder and longer than Konner's quip warranted. But it was the first time I'd laughed since I could remember, and like someone who hasn't driven a car in a long time, I was still getting used to the accelerator and brake.

We clanked our glasses in a toast.

"I don't feel like getting up early tomorrow," I said.

"Me neither."

Some of the staff came over with their palm-leaf fans, but we waved them away. I finished the beer in my glass and leaned forward. "I want to go to Bangan," I half-whispered.

"That place is the most amazing thing I've seen," Konner whispered back. He refilled my glass.

We drank in silence.

"We could just leave," I whispered.

"What about Tommy? He won't go." He eyed me carefully.

"He's a big boy." My voice was strong, defiant. I could do this.

Konner called the waiter over. "We'd like to take a boat back to Sittwe in the morning. Is that possible?"

"Just a moment, sir. I will check."

"Wouldn't it be funny?" Konner said. "Tommy wakes up and we're gone."

"His plans," I said. "All screwed up. Even the *Lonely Planet* won't help him."

We laughed together and ordered two more beers. The waiter returned with the news that the boat left at five in the morning. Our driver would be waiting to take us at four-thirty.

Konner glanced at his watch. "I think I'll get a bit of sleep. Do you want to come?" I wasn't sure what he was proposing. I only knew that I wasn't ready for it.

"You go ahead." I was getting drunk. Konner stood up and staggered toward our room. Tommy was about to get shafted. It felt good to be mean.

I heard a voice like music behind me, and I turned to see the matriarch again. She was speaking rapidly to her two daughters. Their heads were lowered, as if they had done something to displease her. I wondered if they'd upset her on purpose. Either way, I was certain she would forgive them.

I drank alone until the restaurant closed. I sat at my table, the last tourist, while the two remaining waiters busied themselves with the rituals of closing: blowing out candles, picking up bottles, emptying ashtrays.

The air, thick and formless, guided me to my room. In the front area Konner snored on his back, the covers thrown off, wearing only his leopard-patterned bikini underwear (a European thing, I supposed). I watched his hard small belly rise and fall in the moonlight. I tiptoed to the back. Tommy, in his T-shirt and boxers, was on his stomach, his arm stretched out to the spot where I usually slept. The *Lonely Planet* and a stack of Post-It notes were beside his travel alarm clock, which was set for six-thirty. I loosened the silver ring from my wedding finger and placed it next to the clock. I wondered if this was how my father had left my mother, wordlessly, without warning, leaving only his wedding band on the dresser for her to understand everything. I wondered if he felt as I did then, as I had when I had left her myself, guilty, but more than that, breathless with the possibility of escape. I stuffed my bathroom kit and remaining clothes in my backpack and walked out to the restaurant terrace before I changed my mind.

Vinh's car was parked in the road in front of the guesthouse, barely visible under the night sky. I tip-toed over, barefoot, and peered in the passenger window where he was sleeping. His head rested on the steering wheel on his folded arms. He held the photo of his family loosely in his hand.

I sat on the terrace steps and gazed at the sky that stretched far and wide, the stars like jewels on a crown. My stomach hurt and my eyes watered at the sky's implacable beauty that had been hiding from me for so long.

Konner emerged from our room a little after four, bleary-eyed and hung-over. We sat on the steps of the terrace while he smoked. Then we paid the bill and two young men carried our bags to the car, where Vinh stood now, awake and waiting.

I sat in the front with Vinh. We were all silent in the car, subdued by the world of the sleeping. I didn't want to look at him, to have the real-life Vinh, married, perhaps a bit dull and coarse, interfere with my fantasy Vinh, the man who would love me with a passion that cancelled out everything else, for that moment at least.

At the pier Vinh gave us both pieces of paper creased in half. For the rest of my two weeks in Burma I kept the paper in my passport folded, unread, so that I could pretend it held a secret message just for me. Sometimes the message said: *I will never forget you.* Other times it said: *You are not alone.* Usually it said: *All is forgiven.*

Konner and I sat on the floor of the boat as forgiveness floated up and disappeared into the constellation of stars. There was a crunch of gravel and I looked back at the pier. At first I was afraid it was Tommy coming to take me back, but then I saw the two daughters from Max Sunshine emerge from the car and then the matriarch herself, dressed in an emerald *longhi* and a cropped fur coat. The daughters were sluggish in their elastic pants, but the matriarch stepped on the boat with the grace of a blueblood. She was going to Sittwe to visit her son, the proverbial Max Sunshine himself, and check on the accounting books. Her daughters barked orders to a few men who hefted baskets, no doubt filled with food and provisions, onto the boat. The matriarch said little but waved her hand occasionally to indicate where she wanted the baskets.

Once the boat started moving, I closed my eyes until Konner shook me awake for the sunrise, which was unfolding like the plant I had touched near the lotus pond, except in reverse. The fishermen in their boats were covered in a dusky glow that held the promise of the day ahead. I rubbed my hands over my arms from the morning chill. Konner unbuttoned his long-sleeve shirt and wrapped it around my shoulders. He wore only the T-shirt Vinh had given him, but he didn't seem to mind the cool morning air.

He lit a cigarette and handed it to me.

"What are you thinking?" he asked in a way that sounded like he really meant it.

"I was thinking of my mother. She died almost two years ago. Car accident. I wasn't the best daughter." I inhaled deeply before passing the cigarette back to him. I hadn't smoked one since I'd left Korea, and it felt sharp and invigorating.

"I'm sorry," Konner said softly. He took my hand.

"You never seemed this nice before."

"You look so fragile. I don't know why I didn't see it earlier. I should have."

With my free hand I held the shirt tightly around my shoulders.

Sitting at the front of the boat was the matriarch, her back erect, her fur coat clasped around her throat. A few wisps of hair had fallen loose from her bun and blew against her delicate cheekbones and long, slender neck. In another world she would have been a fifties film star or an heiress. She knew how much everyone, especially her daughters, loved and feared her and that she was still the most beautiful person in the land.

The matriarch smiled broadly at me. She placed her hands together in prayer and lowered her head slightly. Then her mouth reverted to its naturally regal expression. Like an ageless queen she resumed her watch, commander and protector of all that was in her realm.

GRAPE ISLAND

She wrote him during the rainy season in Bangkok, with its flooded streets, umbrella wars, and mangy dying dogs huddled against fences and walls. From her tiny apartment window she watched the Thais, soaked, yet Buddha-like, going about their business, unaffected by the weather. Elise herself had so far failed to achieve that state of grace.

Four years ago, she had left him sleeping in her grandfather's pea coat in the Korean love hotel. That was the last time she had seen the coat or him. She still had his parents' address, though, a scrap of paper folded in the crease of her wallet. He had lived there when they'd been lovers, and she assumed he lived there now, as was the duty of eldest sons. More than a year into the new millennium, a letter seemed quaint and old fashioned, but, she thought, that was what their love had been as well.

Dear Danny,

I am writing because I would like you to return the coat I left with you. I am moving back to the States soon, and will need it for the cold weather. Also, the coat has sentimental value as you know.

I have a 12-hour layover in Seoul next month on my way back to the States. If you can leave the coat at the airport I would appreciate it.

She paused. The pen hovered in midair. Her hand shook as she wrote the next part.

I hope you have found happiness with the wife and children you and your parents wanted.

Sincerely, Elise

A few weeks later, Elise received a letter from Danny. His handwriting was neatly formed in the way that people who have practiced a foreign language write: learned, careful, exact.

Dear Elise,

I was so shocked and happy to receive your letter. I will pick you up at the airport and drive you to the countryside. We will talk about old times there. I have been keeping your coat safely and will return it to you. Do you have email? Please write to me at the email address below. It is much faster.

Yours truly, Danny

There was no mention of a wife or children. Surely he must have them, she thought. There could be a hundred different reasons why he didn't mention them in his letter. He would tell her when he saw her. She wrote him a brief email, and they agreed he would meet her at the Seoul airport next Thursday.

She didn't recognize Danny at first, but he held a large piece of paper with her name etched in dark marker, so she knew it must be him, this man in a suit, with hair like a Brillo pad. He was heavier, too, although not overweight by western standards. His face looked fuller, his body softer. She had forgotten how quickly Korean men aged once they became salarymen. She had failed to adjust her memory of him from five years ago: the lean, muscled arms under his tight T-shirt, the wide, full-lipped smile, and later, his coiled, naked body in one of the love hotels that had been their escape.

"It's good to see you," she said as they shook hands. She was relieved that his touch did not bring back the sharp wanting from that time.

"Me, too." Danny smiled. It was an imitation of the smile that had first drawn her to him, a smile that was large, genuine, and spontaneous. The smile held the same form, but now it seemed forced, with no feeling behind its shape. Elise wondered, had the smile changed, or merely her response to it?

They left the airport, and Danny exited onto the expressway. She soon realized that, in Korean fashion, they wouldn't talk about what had happened between them for a while, and she was okay with that. He told her that he used to work in a bank but that now he was a social worker and was taking her with him to check on his cases, mostly the poor, orphaned, and elderly. Then he asked her about Thailand.

"It's been good to me." She told him she'd traveled around Southeast Asia for a year after leaving Seoul, and then settled into life in Bangkok, teaching children English at a private school. Even in the rainy season she hated leaving Bangkok—the curries, the temples, the hot, steamy streets, the river boat taxis, and of course the Thais themselves, their smiles like sudden gifts from a God still unknown to her.

Danny pulled onto the expressway, then glanced at her as she struggled to find the seatbelt. "You still look young. Me, I'm old man." He smiled slightly.

"You look fine. Like a salaryman." After successfully digging out the seatbelt, she fastened it. "Where's your earring?"

"Pardon?"

She started to reach out to his ear where the gold hoop earring he had once worn had been, but pulled her hand back toward her own earlobe.

"Oh yes. Sorry. My English is terrible. I forget many things," he said. He reached and touched his ear. "Earring is for college boy."

"Do you still live with your parents?"

"Yes. My mother take care of my daughter."

"So you do have a child! How old is she?"

"Korean age is four, American age, three."

"Can I meet her?"

"Oh no. Not possible."

Elise nodded. Of course: not possible. The traffic had started to thin as they left the city.

"What about your wife?" She hoped her voice sounded casual.

Danny was silent. He squinted his eyes as if a harsh sun were on him, although the day was overcast. "After I lose my job at the bank, she run away. Now we divorce."

"Oh, Danny. I'm sorry." Elise rested her head back and closed her eyes. "I didn't even know Koreans got divorced."

"Before, no. But now, after the economic crisis, it is

common."

Elise opened her eyes and glanced at him. His eyes were open again, keeping vigilance on the constant lane changing and stops and starts of the traffic. His lips pressed together, as if he wanted to tell her something, but thought better of it.

"What about you?" he finally asked. "Are you married?"

Elise shook her head.

"Is that why you are going back to America? To marry? Have a baby?"

Elise laughed and told him no. She told him she was happy alone.

"Alone is not good. I know."

"I'm okay. Don't worry."

"So why are you going back?"

"It just feels like time." She pressed her head against the window pane. Since she'd left Seoul at the end of 1996, Korea had experienced economic collapse followed by a rocky but miraculous recovery. Even more miraculously, the Koreans had elected a former dissident and future Nobel Peace Prize winner to be president. With that she had expected changes. Yet as she stared out the window, all Elise could see were apartments, the same as before, but more of them, distinguished only by the numbers painted on the side of each building. Elise thought things had probably not changed much at all.

They drove in silence until they reached a concrete bridge. Danny told her they were driving to a place called Grape Island.

"Sounds magical," Elise said.

"It's not really an island, though," Danny said.

Grape Island had been a small island at one time, but

was now connected to and absorbed by the mainland through a network of roads and bridges. As they crossed the bridge, Elise noted the flat-roofed houses dotting the rolling hills and fields of farmland. Elise felt they had stepped back in time to an idyllic, if not idealized, Korean way of life that had been lost in Seoul: a life of a slower rhythm sustained by the land and the livelihood it brought.

Narrow, concrete roads wound them around the town. They were surrounded by fields full of grapes, ripened, and ready to be eaten. Danny stopped the car and returned with a swollen bunch of grapes straight off the vine.

"I will find good place to eat these," he said. As he drove away from the village, the houses were spaced farther apart, and the concrete road turned to dirt. He steered onto a narrow road, which seemed to lead to more grape fields and fewer houses.

"Do you have my coat?" The question had bubbled out of her unexpectedly, surprising even Elise with its urgency.

"In the back." He gestured stiffly with one hand to the trunk.

She nodded. She wanted to jump out of the car, grab the coat, and put it on.

The car dipped suddenly, scraping against something hard and sharp.

Danny said he was sorry and continued driving. They both pretended nothing had happened. After a half mile, the car seized. He turned the ignition a few times, but the engine wouldn't start. Outside of the car, they saw their fate in the neon-green antifreeze spreading along the dirt road, like an alien that had lost solid form. She knew it was irrational, but Elise felt that Danny had done this on purpose.

After he called a towing company on his cellular phone, Danny led her to an abandoned house not far from the road. Elise thought it strange that this old house would be there, so conveniently for them, and she again irrationally wondered if Danny had set the whole thing up, had somehow caused the accident just so he could take her here. But why would he do that, she wondered. It didn't make sense.

The house, at least fifty years old, was built in the traditional style, square-shaped with a yard in the middle for cooking and washing clothes. They strolled along the walkway, looking into each room. When they reached the kitchen, Danny pointed to the space in the ground under the floor, which was where the fire went for cooking and heat, as there was no electricity. The rooms were small and had sliding doors covered with rice paper. Danny poked his finger through the paper.

"People make a hole here to watch a honeymoon couple on their wedding night," he said. "Old tradition."

Elise thought of the secret times they had spent in the love hotels in Seoul, and wondered if he was thinking of that, too. They peered from room to room, each one a repetition of the last, faded and empty.

"This house is the old way," Danny said. "We don't live like this anymore."

She'd been to Danny's parents' house once, and she remembered its sleek western appliances, even an oven for show that his mother used to store her pots and pans in, leather sofas, and oak bedroom sets nicer than anything she'd grown up with. She wondered if he thought she'd forgotten all that, and it was his duty to remind her.

They sat on the wooden walkway that surrounded the house. The clouds were darkening and threatened rain. Danny took out a pack of cigarettes and pointed them in her direction.

"Thanks, but I quit," Elise said.

"Good." He took a cigarette and lit it. "Better for health."

After Danny finished his cigarette, he walked to the car and came back with a bottle and two paper cups and a large bunch of grapes.

"*Soju*." Elise laughed as he unscrewed the cap. A rice alcohol, *soju* was the most popular drink in Korea because it was cheap and potent.

He filled their paper cups to the brim. "Bottoms up," he said and tossed back the cup. Elise squeezed her eyes and downed the drink. It burned her throat and her eyes watered.

"Still *soju*," she said.

"Good taste," Danny said and poured again. He drained his in one motion while Elise held hers in her hand and waited for him to speak. Drinking in Korea usually meant confessions. "Maybe we will have to wait a long time for the truck."

Elise plucked a grape, squeezed the tip and popped the flesh out of its skin into her mouth. The grapes were dark, almost black, full of seeds, and achingly sweet. She added the thick skin to a pile Danny had started.

Danny looked at the ground. "The coat is your grandfather's," he said. "From our war."

"Yes."

"Did he die here?"

"No. He died many years later. In the States."

"You never told me. I feel like a fool." He flicked his cigarette butt away from them.

"Please don't," Elise said. "I just felt strange about it."

He took another cigarette out of the pack and lit it. He drained his cup of *soju,* and let Elise refill it for him as a way of apology.

"I had a good job, at the bank, a real salaryman. After the economic crisis, I lost it, like many people. This job is not so good. My wife ran away to Canada."

"Your wife. Is she the one I saw you with, before?"

Danny's forehead wrinkled. "No. I married someone else. Big mistake."

"You have your daughter at least."

Danny shrugged. "What good is that with no mother? Every day I see other people's troubles. Every night I drink and cry about my own. I am lonely."

Elise touched his shoulder. "You won't always be."

They sipped their *soju* in silence.

"Sometimes I think about us," Danny finally said, his voice soft. "I was very foolish."

"Me too."

"I regret," he said in a low voice.

Elise grabbed his hand and squeezed it briefly before letting go. "It would have been a mistake."

He took out another cigarette. "Life here is very hard."

"Life is hard everywhere." She picked up a grape and squeezed its juice and flesh into her mouth, savoring its sweetness. The air was thick with the sticky grapes and the promise of rain.

"You were my first true love," he said.

She knew what he meant. For Koreans first love was

everything. For him, she was a container for all that had been lost and all that could have been.

"I want to remember the past with you. Make another memory." This time he drank directly from the bottle before passing it to Elise. As she put the bottle to her lips, she was sure she tasted him.

Danny leaned into her, as if he were about to tell her a secret. He breathed *soju* and Korean cigarettes onto her. "I want to go to America with you."

"What about your daughter?"

"She is better without me."

"No," she said sharply. "You cannot leave her."

He was crying now, with the same squinted eyes she had seen in the car. She put her arm around him. "You cannot leave her," she said again.

Her touch this time took them back to that old place. He threw himself on top of her, and for a moment she felt warm, protected. The wooden boards bit as she lay back on the walkway, her legs still dangling over. She heard the *soju* bottle roll off the ledge. Her mouth covered his. She grabbed the short stubble of his hair, and once again she was buried in the secret of their love, which, because it was unseen and unknown from the world, was somehow perfect and always new.

That was the problem with first loves. Too perfect. The days of sharing cake in the cafés, passing a bottle of beer on the shop steps well past midnight, kissing furtively on darkened side streets, his arms around her, a blanket around both of them, the intensity of sex, naked and wet on the warm floors—those days were gone. She thought of his parents and his duty to take care of them, and then his daughter, how she needed her father.

Danny's body felt sluggish and heavy on her, the *soju* and cigarettes now hot and acrid on her face. She shook her head away from his kisses and pushed him.

"No," she said.

He kept kissing her.

"No. Really." She pushed him harder than she had intended. He rolled off the walkway into the muddy ground.

"Shit," he said.

She stood up, and strode away from him toward the road.

"I want to go home," Elise whimpered. She had not been home in a very long time.

As if on cue, an old man walking down the road stopped at the sound of Elise's voice. He yelled and raised his cane. With his long beard and traditional *hanbok*, he looked like a Korean from another era. Elise wondered if he had come from the past to save her.

Danny brushed the mud off his suit and yelled a greeting back. He ran up to the man and bowed slightly. They talked animatedly. The man looked at Elise, then circled the car as Danny continued to talk. The man pointed down the dirt road with his cane. Danny walked back, picked the *soju* bottle out of the mud and placed it in his suit pocket, then in large dramatic motions, wiped the remaining mud off his pants and jacket.

"We will go to his house now." His voice was toneless.

"What about the tow truck?"

"Maybe it is not coming. I have to call again. We had better wait at his house."

"I'm going to miss my flight." Her voice tightened, and she thought she might cry.

He took out a piece of paper from his coat pocket and punched some numbers on the cell phone. He removed his wallet from his back pocket then turned away from her. He bobbed with each grunted affirmation before hanging up. He slid the wallet back and shifted so that he was facing her, although he did not look up from the ground.

"I made reservation at a hotel near the airport tonight. You can fly tomorrow. I will pay." As she stepped toward him he raised his palm like a policeman stopping traffic. "My mistake."

She smiled thinly to reassure him. They were going to pretend to forget.

The old man lived with his wife and granddaughter in a three-room house down the street from where the car had broken down. The granddaughter was one of Danny's social work cases. Her parents had died in a car accident when she was five.

The girl had unusually large, dark eyes. She was eleven years old and greeted Elise with a nod that was smothered under her grandmother's curled arm. Elise looked at the girl, shy, vulnerable, but somehow also open, and the thought flashed like an unbidden vision: in another life, this girl could be me, or my mother, or my daughter. Danny and I could have had a daughter who would have grown up to look like her, a girl with my eyes and his smile. Or if back there I had let him, there might be the seed of a child, our child, just beginning, and we could start a new family and try to do things right. The vision vanished as quickly as it had appeared. That is not this life, she thought.

They sat on the floor of the main room. A narrow kitchen was set off from them and an opened door led to an empty room where the family slept. A TV with rabbit ears and two knobs was centered on top a wooden box. Above the TV an oval mirror, its thin glass rubbed down to a black sheen hung from a rusted nail. Tied to the mirror with a piece of grubby string was a black plastic comb. The old man opened a large bottle of beer and poured some into the glasses. Danny and the man spoke in Korean. Elise sipped her beer and watched the girl, who sat near the entrance to the kitchen, ready to do her grandmother's bidding. After about ten minutes, the grandmother emerged with a tray full of bowls of rice, soup of red pepper and slices of beef, and *kimchi*. Once they began eating Elise realized how hungry she was.

"He want to speak English to you," Danny said. "He could speak a little after the war. But that was long time ago, and he forgot it."

"That's okay," Elise said, smiling at the man.

"He graduated from high school. At that time most people didn't do that."

The men talked more. The girl went to the kitchen and returned with more side dishes and beer. Everyone's glasses were refilled, and they made a toast. Danny said something to the man and they both looked at her. The old man pushed himself off the floor and stepped toward Elise. He extended his hand. She took it and he shook her hand vigorously.

"I told him your grandfather fought in the war," Danny said.

"Thank you," the old man said. He put his other hand on top of hers. Elise nodded, unsure of what to say. The old man sat down and refilled everyone's glasses. He made another toast.

"The old generation, they are thankful to America," Danny said. "But my generation, we don't believe that. We know America doesn't care about us. His son was killed in Vietnam. Why? Because America use us."

He stared at her, and she stared back. If they had been alone, if it were five years ago, they would have fought then, clawed and scratched each other until they'd collapsed from exhaustion. She felt the girl's eyes on them, and Elise turned to her. The girl jumped up and ran into the kitchen. Elise wanted to follow her; instead she stayed rooted on the floor.

The old man continued to talk animatedly. Danny nodded but said little in response.

"He says it is fate that we come here, because of our past," Danny finally said. He finished his drink and excused himself to call the tow truck. The girl brought in a plate full of grapes and a stack of packaged cookies along with a sweet rice drink for dessert. She sat down nearer to the table with a notebook that she began to write in. After a few minutes, Elise stood up to step outside. As she walked out, she saw that the girl was writing English words in her notebook. *House. Chair. Book.*

"What is this?" Elise opened her hand that held a grape in it.

The girl looked up, startled, and shrank back. She shook her head.

"Grape," Elise said. "Here." She held the grape out for the girl to take. The girl closed her book. Elise centered the grape on the girl's notebook and walked outside.

Danny paced under the slope of the roof and smoked a cigarette while talking rapidly into his cell phone. When he saw Elise, he finished his conversation and hung up. The tow truck driver had changed his mind, he told her. There was too much traffic on the bridge and he had found someone closer who needed his help.

"Sometimes, I hate this country." Danny turned away from her and looked out at the night in front of them.

She stood behind him and spoke loud enough so he could hear her.

"What's that Korean word? Not the one that means sadness and longing. Another one. You told me once. Affection. Bond. Bondage. Hard to let go."

"You mean *jung*."

"That's it." Her body ached with something that was bigger than love or loss. She spread her hands before her, pale webs that skimmed his back so softly he didn't feel them. She wanted to grab his hands and hold them until his bones ached. Instead, she dropped her hands to her side. She looked back in the house. The girl was wiping the table where they had eaten.

"Could you give me the address to this place? I'd like to write the girl when I get back to the States." Elise would write the letters that she had wanted to get from her father, letters that talked about food and weather, but also asked and answered the other questions: How are you feeling today? Do you miss your parents? Who do you love at this moment?

"Danny."

He faced her, took out a scrap of paper and pen from his inside suit pocket, scribbled the address and handed it to her.

"Her name is Kim Ji Hyun. And my name isn't Danny. It's Young Soo." He walked back inside.

She folded the paper into a square and tucked it in her wallet where she had kept his parents' address for so many years. Elise stood in the dark for another minute, her hand shaking. She wanted to remember how it felt to love him.

She looked for the moon or a few stars, but they were covered in clouds. Elise thought she understood why the Thais embraced the rain. They believed your karma followed you until you faced it and accepted it as your own.

The grandfather called one of the farmers who had a truck. The farmer would hook up the car to his truck and take them over the bridge. It was going to be a long ride, with Elise and Young Soo in the car being slowly towed back over the bridge off the island. From there she could get a taxi to a hotel near the airport, where all could be recovered in a night's sleep. Young Soo, on the other hand, had work the next day, his parents, a daughter, a ghost wife, a broken car, and the weight of the new memories that would reshape the remembering. She envied him. Soon she would be back in the States searching for a place where she could cultivate attachments of her own.

When the farmer arrived, they all walked down the street in the darkness to the car sunk in the mud. The antifreeze had already washed away in the rain. Young Soo opened the trunk and removed a large plastic bag. He handed Elise the bag without a word, but she didn't take it.

"It's yours," she said. "For real this time."

He held the bag suspended above the wet ground. He could drop it there and walk away. She knew he was considering it. Instead, his arm went slack and he bowed slightly. Young Soo took the pea coat out of the bag and slipped it on, even though winter was still months away. The sleeves were unrolled and he folded the cuffs up, as

Elise had also once done, so that the coat fit him.

Elise walked back to Ji Hyun and the grandmother. They watched the men test the chain by pulling the car a few feet. The rain had stopped, and the night was wet and cool. Elise felt something on her arm, as light as a butterfly. Ji Hyun pointed to where the clouds had parted. The night sky stretched endlessly before them, unknown and unbidden, beyond attachment and suffering. It must have given them both the courage to speak.

"Look," Ji Hyun said. "*Dahl. Byul. Hana.*"

Elise held on tightly to the girl's warm hand.

"I remember. I remember," Elise whispered. "Moon. Star. Sky."

ACKNOWLEDGEMENTS

Thanks to Chad, Ryan, and Jamie, and all the folks at C&R for being such an awesome press; to my parents, Arlene and Calvin Baker, to my brothers, Burton and Derek, to the sisters I never had, Stefanie and Ozgur; to my South African family, Lee, Lorraine, and Kyle; to the wonderful writers, mentors, and teachers who worked with me on this collection at different stages of its development: Robert Eversz, Nance Van Winkle, Patricia Henley, Abby Frucht, David Jauss, and Xu Xi; to the MFA program at Vermont College of Fine Arts, especially Louise Crowley, Robin Hemley, and Richard Jackson; to Sarah for her amazing photographs; to the fabulous Katie Christie, publicist and writer extraordinaire; to Silvia Tartarini who helped me so much with early versions of the manuscript but didn't live to see its published form; to Silvia's sister Cinzia for keeping Silvia's spirit alive; and to Rowan, as always, for everything.

Some of the stories in this book first appeared in slightly different form in the following publications:
Owen Wister Review ("Firefly"), *Motif: Writing by Ear* (Motes Books) ("Tempo"), *RE:AL* ("That Girl" as "The Navy Pea Coat"), *Transnational Literature* ("Talismans"), *Slow Trains* ("Picturing Snakes"), *The Bitter Oleander* ("Blue"), *Paper Street* ("The Ice Queen"), *The Willow Review* ("Grape Island").

Cover photo by Sarah Hadley
Cover & Interior redesign by Lee Johnson

TALISMANS

TALISMANS

CPSIA information can be obtained
at www.ICGtesting.com
Printed in the USA
BVOW08s1425191217
503203BV00001B/151/P